Trigger Gospel

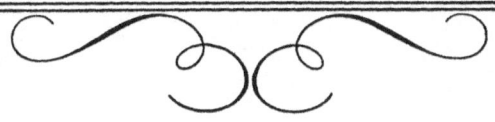

By

SINCLAIR DRAGO

Author of
"Desert Water," "Guardians of the Sage," etc.

M. EVANS
Essex, Connecticut

M. Evans
An imprint of The Globe Pequot Publishing Group, Inc.
64 South Main Street
Essex, CT 06426
www.globepequot.com

Library of Congress Cataloging-in-Publication Data Available

ISBN 13: 978-1-59077-487-8 (pbk)

For

EDWARD A. DUCKER
Justice of
The Supreme Court of Nevada

Whose feet have trod the lonely cañons and
wind-swept rimrocks, where a man's
best companion is himself.

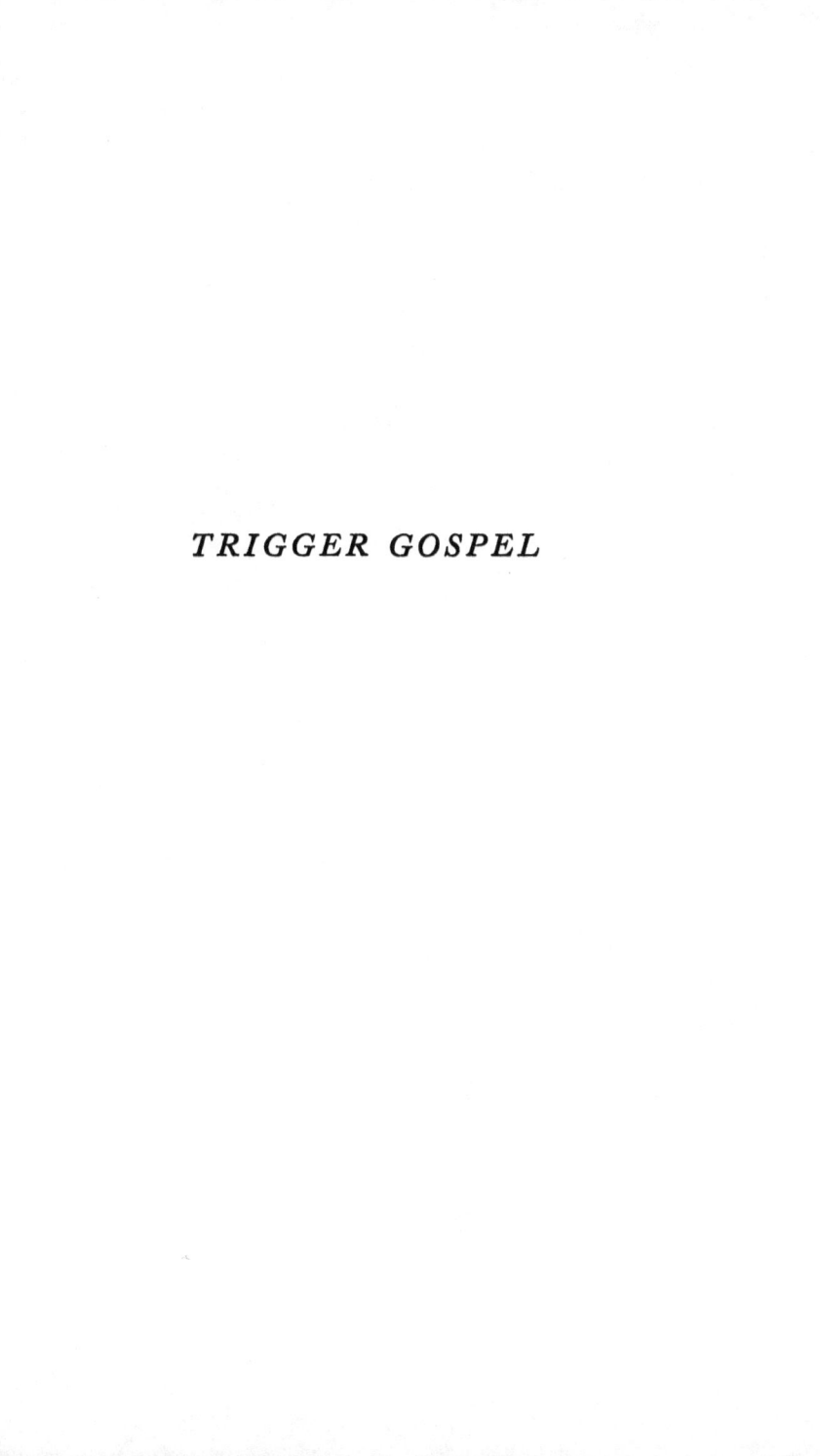

TRIGGER GOSPEL

Chapter I

WHEN Dodge City was the end of steel for the whole South West, the thundering hoofs of a million Texas longhorns carved deep into the prairie sod of Oklahoma the trail that old Tascosa Cummings and his little X Bar X spread followed this long, hot July afternoon.

Thirty years had passed since the last of the great trail herds had come bawling up from the Panhandle. Those ghostly legions of longhorns and the brawling, reckless men of that all-but-forgotten day lived now only in the memories of such old-timers as himself. Even the trail, packed down with their sweat and blood, had been all but effaced by the jungle-like growth of native bluejoint grass that grew saddle-high on the rolling plains between the North Fork of the Canadian and the Cimarron.

And yet, Tascosa, riding at the head of his outfit, followed it without conscious effort as it uncoiled its tawny, rutted ribbon to the north. He had nothing to say, but the old trail stirred vagrant emotions in him, and he screwed his long, thin, weather-beaten face into a flinty squint that almost hid his faded blue eyes.

"Almost gone," he told himself sadly. "She ain't waiting to be ploughed under. Another year or two and there won't be nothin' left—nary a sign to say this was once the hell-roarin'est boulevard on earth."

The blotting out of the old Texas trail was but one of many evidences of social decay that he professed to see in the Oklahoma that had grown up under his very nose, so to speak. Seventy, if he was a day, a product of the era of the free-range when men roamed the plains high, wide and handsome, he had only a withering contempt for the nester who was satisfied to dig in on a little two-by-four patch of a hundred and sixty acres of government land and call it a ranch, and he had but little more respect for the new generation of cowmen, boxed off with barbed wire, who spouted new-fangled nonsense about improving the blood strains of their stock and doubling the weight of a steer.

He now expressed his disgust for the pack of them with a grunt that was as eloquent as it was profane. He spat out the cud of tobacco that had served him for hours.

"Progress! Improvements!" he snorted fiercely. "Damn their souls, that's what's ruinin' this yere country. They got her all broken down in the loins already with their town sites and lightnin' rods. Gittin' so a man can't turn around this side of the Nations or the Strip without stumbling over somebody. If it keeps on it'll soon be a crime to even pack a gun here."

Considering that at the moment Oklahoma was overrun with outlaws; that Bowie, a division point on the Rock Island Pacific, was the only town west of Kingfisher; that there was not a foot of made road nor a doctor, preacher or lawyer (working at his trade) in ten thousand square miles of territory; that to all practical purposes the six-gun was still the popular arbiter of right and wrong, made it appear that Tascosa was unduly apprehensive.

Of course, it was a subject on which he was not only biased but in certain quarters held to be just a little cracked. Certainly he was a disreputable old hooker, dirty, lawless and as full of guile as a Kiowa halfbreed. In the way of the old days, he wore his hair long, and at those rare moments when he removed his battered Stetson, he looked like nothing so much as a scrawny, tobacco-stained old eagle.

His X Bar X brand—always called the old Sawbuck —had not decorated a steer's hide in ten years. His chuck wagon was his ranch house. And yet he was prosperous, for he made a business of bidding on the government beef issues to the tribes down in the Nations. With a signed contract in his pocket, he would start looking for cattle. Sometimes he went incredible distances, but he usually succeeded in doing business on his own terms before he closed. The long drive to one of the agencies followed. He had to be there on time, hell or high water, and he always was. Then lazy days until it was time to repeat the operation.

It was a nomadic, care-free existence that suited him better than anything else he could have devised. Its lack of restraint, its breath of danger and excitement, the dash of hard work and the sure promise of long periods of ease made it something utterly desirable in other eyes than his, and he had drawn unto himself half-a-dozen men cut after his own pattern—hard-riding, two-fisted fighting men who could lick three times their weight or numbers with fist or gun as the occasion demanded.

They were on their way up from Anadarko and the Kiowa country now, heading back to Bowie. Behind them, well back out of the dust their ponies were kicking up, rumbled the wagon, with Maverick Williams, the cook, asleep on the seat and seemingly certain to be pitched out on his face at every jolt. Skull Creek was their destination for the night. They had been rambling along since dawn, and when Tascosa flung up his hand a few minutes later and signaled that the creek was in sight, they answered with a sharp yip of satisfaction and spurred up to where he waited at the top of the rise. Below them, off to the right a few hundred yards, a dense tangle of willow and wild cherry marked the course of the Skull.

"Thar she is boys!" Tascosa declared. "We used to drive right down to the stream years ago; but it sure looks as though a twister had torn things up around here just recent. Suppose you all spread out and find a way to git the wagon down. Me and Little Bill will jest follow the old trail to the bottom of this yere slope and see what that little draw looks like."

"Well, come on, let's ramble," Little Bill jerked out. "The shadows are gettin' long."

He was a little runt of a man, not over five feet four even in his high-heeled boots, and the rangy claybank gelding that he rode, at least three hands higher than any horse in the outfit, made him appear even smaller than he was. His hands and feet were as tiny as a woman's. It was an incongruous touch, for although he was still under thirty there was something in the depths of his hazel eyes and the reckless set of his mouth that said he was a human buzz-saw when aroused. Shrewd, habitually alert, he had made himself Tascosa's lieutenant and over others, his elder brother Luther included, who had been riding for the Sawbuck for years. Without waiting for old Tas, he sank his knees into his big horse and started down the trail. His brother Luther and the others struck off across the slope. The old man had to use his spurs to overtake him.

"Say, what's the rush?" he demanded crustily.

"I ain't aimin' to go pokin' around no creek bottom after dark," Little Bill answered. "We might run onto some folks that prefer their own company."

"Dark? Why the sun's an hour high yet!"

"It won't be if we don't find water here and have to go on to the Cimarron."

"Right," old Tas acknowledged gruffly. Experience had taught him that Little Bill was usually right, even though he made a virtue of never admitting it.

They reached the bottom of the hill and began to pick their way down the draw, with Little Bill in the lead. He had not progressed over thirty yards when he pulled up abruptly to stare at something on the ground.

"What is it?" Tascosa whipped out as he saw him freeze to attention. For answer, Little Bill pointed to a bare, sandy spot in the jungle of grass.

"Fresh tracks of shod horses," he said. "They ain't over an hour old. Five or six in that bunch."

"Jest about." Tascosa thoughtfully masticated a fresh chew of tobacco. "Headin' for the creek too. Didn't notice no tracks cuttin' across the trail."

"Neither did I," Little Bill agreed. "Reckon they was careful not to leave any. The grass ain't broken down neither. That's tellin' me plenty." His manner was suddenly grave.

"Yeh?" The old man narrowed his eyes and squirted a stream of tobacco juice with expert aim at a blue beetle. "What do you figger it means, Bill?"

The question was beside the point, for he understood him perfectly. The intentness with which he was scanning the tree-choked creek bottom proved it.

"The same as you," Little Bill snapped. "Long riders; somebody sneakin' out of the Strip on unfinished business. Not over two hundred and fifty yards to the creek. Reckon they got us covered this minute with a high-power or two."

"Like as not," Tas muttered grimly. The words were hardly out of his mouth before the bark of a .30-.30 shattered the stillness of early evening. "Well," he grunted as the echo rolled down the creek, "that's language I can understand. We ain't lost no banks nor express boxes, so we'll just back-trail outa here pronto."

He stood up in his stirrups and hailed his men with a shrill cry.

Five minutes later they were back on the trail. The wagon had come up too.

"What was that shootin'?" Maverick cried out.

"The Skull is too crowded for us tonight," Tascosa explained soberly. "We're goin' on to the Cimarron. We'll have to step along right lively to make it afore sundown. You shake up that team, Maverick; we're movin'!"

Chapter II

TASCOSA and his five men rode abreast. They traded questions.

"Who do you figure they are?" Luther Stillings drawled casually. He had his brother's freckles and brick-red hair. In no other way were they alike, save in their promise of efficiency in a pinch.

"The Doolins—or maybe Smoke Sontag," Little Bill answered. "It's about time for the Sontags to be breakin' loose again."

"That's sumthin' for the marshals and sheriffs to worry about," Tascosa reminded them. "It ain't our put-in no way at all. We h'ain't seen a thing."

"I hope to tell yuh we ain't," Link Appling grinned. "It's strictly a two-sided fight. Just part your hair in the middle, boys, and don't lean one way or t'other."

"You're dead right, Link," Scotty Ryan, the dean of Tascosa's hired hands agreed. "It t'ain't no shine off our pants no matter what happens. See nothin', say nothin' and you may live to a ripe old age, unless Maverick's cookin' kills you afore your time."

They laughed, and there was no dissenting opinion, for Link and Scotty had only expressed a viewpoint that was typical of the attitude of their calling. Honest themselves, they never knew when they might drift into

outlawry. Certainly most of those who rode with Red
Doolin and Smoke Sontag had once been cowboys.
They still had friends, legions of them, or else the law
would have turned them up in a hurry. An outsider
wouldn't have understood this bond between good men
and bad, nor been able to find any definite line of de-
marcation between those inside the law and out, for
the bad and good in them was sadly scrambled.

Little Bill set the pace. He was inclined to run away
from the wagon. There was no point in that. He
looked back to see Maverick dozing again.

"I'll start his circulation a hoppin'!" he ground out
furiously. "He's got somethin' on his hip."

He dropped back until he rode abreast the wagon.
He didn't bother to shout to Maverick, but drawing
one of his brass-handled .45's sent a slug crashing into
the bottle that protruded from the cook's hip pocket.
Maverick jerked his two hundred and ten pounds of
fat erect as though he worked on wires.

"Why, you red-headed little ant, I'll eat you alive
for that!" he roared. "Damn you, don't you ever try
to curry me that-a-way! I'll——"

Little Bill emptied his six-gun over the heads of the
weary horses and they leaped away with a rush that cut
short the tirade.

"You high-tail it now, Maverick!" he shouted as the
wagon began to hit only the high places. "I'm layin'
back here to dust you off if you don't!"

There was a twinkle in his eyes, for Maverick and
he were the best of friends.

The rolling hills began to give way to level plain.

They made better time now. Maverick held the team to a steady trot, with the result that the sun was just sliding below the horizon when they rode down into the valley of the Cimarron to bring up a few minutes later at a grassy flat just below Cherokee crossing. Here was wood, water and grass.

In no time at all Maverick had his cook-fire going and his end of the wagon open. He was slicing thick steaks off a butt of beef as Little Bill approached.

"Nice goin'," the red-haired one grinned.

"Yeh?" Maverick growled. "I been pickin' glass outa my backside for ten miles. I hope I git hyderphoby or somethin' so I can give it to you."

"You mean so you can charge me for it; you never gave nothin' away in your ornery old life," Little Bill retorted as he reached under the seat for a currycomb and brush.

He had already watered his horse. The big gelding was picketed on the flat now, and as the others stretched out on the ground, glad to be out of the saddle after the long day, Little Bill got busy with his brush and comb.

Before long the animal's coat began to shine. The horse seemed to enjoy the attention that was being lavished on it. He was a clean-limbed three-year-old with a long barrel; the best proof in the world that there was little if any mustang blood in him.

Absorbed in what he was doing, Little Bill worked on without glancing at the lounging men who, without exception, were watching him with growing interest. He had owned the gelding but a short while, having acquired the horse down in the Panhandle as the result of some shrewd trading and the spending of the better part of his bankroll. His pride in the animal and the care he lavished on it had already resulted in an inordinate amount of chaffing at his expense, and the present moment was pregnant with fresh possibilities. Link Appling fired the first gun a few moments later.

"Too bad a high-falutin' critter like that has to be bogged down with a common, cow pony name like Six-gun," he declared, addressing Tonto Baker. "You been below the Rio Grande and you savvy them tony Mexican names, Tonto. Why don't you suggest somethin' fittin' to Bill?"

"Well, there might be something to that," Tonto replied, putting on a thoughtful face. "But I ain't up much on anythin' but girls' names. You could hardly tack anythin' like Conchita or Estancia on that geldin'. Bill might think I was castin' aspersions."

"I'll do a little castin' myself, and like as not it'll be this currycomb," the red-haired one retorted, "if you start any of your greaser lingo on me."

"There he goes; on the prod already," Link protested. "You can't open your mouth even in a helpful way no more."

The others laughed as he shook his head sadly.

"Now look here; you boys lay off of Bill," old Tas put in with deep cunning, for he enjoyed the fun as much as any. "Bill's got a big impression to make when he rides into Bowie tomorrow mornin'. If I thought for a minute that I was goin' to meet anybody half as sweet as he does I'd begin usin' a currycomb on myself, I'm tellin' yuh!"

"Now I did forget all about that for a fact," Link asserted gravely. "I sure beg your pardon, Bill. You go right ahead and put ribbons in that horse's tail if you want to and it'll be all right with me. But just the same, I think you're takin' a chance in dollin' that animal up that-a-way. I can't speak for the lady, but if it was me, I'd find it a little confusin'; I wouldn't know just which one of you to choose."

"I'd take the horse," Scotty Ryan called out.

"I'm sure you would, Scotty," Little Bill fired back. "A horse and a jackass ought to hit it off pretty good."

The laugh was on Scotty now, and they enjoyed it quite as much as though it had been on Bill. They returned to the attack then and kept at it until Maverick was ready for them. The cook ran a critical eye over the gelding.

"Fly speck there on the right stifle, Bill," he cried. "Take care of that and you can come and get it!"

They ate with a hearty appetite. The purple haze of twilight was beginning to settle down on the river bottom. Little Bill sat beside Tascosa.

"The joshin's over, Bill," said the old man. "The geldin's a fine horse. But sure as fate somebody'll try to steal him. If you'll take my advice you'll sell him. You can get a good price."

"Not a chance," Bill answered bluntly. "Nobody but me is ever goin' to ride him. He's all I ever wanted in a horse, and I'm keepin' him. The hombre that tries to lift him won't live long."

"All right, have it your way," Tas grumbled. "But mark my words; that claybank will make you trouble. I never knew one that wa'n't unlucky."

They had just lit their cigarettes when five mounted men appeared on the skyline across the river and headed for their camp. Luther was the first to see them.

"Make out who they are?" Tascosa demanded anxiously.

"They're ridin' with their rifles across their saddle bows," Little Bill answered, his eyes narrowed on the oncoming horsemen. "It ain't likely it's the bunch we spotted on the Skull. That big fellow in the lead looks familiar."

A moment or two later he recognized the man.

"It's Cash Beaudry, the so-called sheriff of Cimarron County," he sneered.

"It's Beaudry and a bunch of deputies, all right," Luther seconded. "Their broncs look like they'd ridden 'em into the ground."

"Long riders—now the sheriff," Tascosa muttered. "That usually makes sense."

"Not this time," Little Bill rasped. "If Beaudry ever bumps into an outlaw's way it'll be by accident. He's a cheap, double-crossin' crook, accordin' to the record. You know it as well as I do. There's some connection between the Sontags and him, and that's what gravels me—makin' a splurge about runnin' 'em down when he's really trailin' with 'em."

"I've heard it, but I don't know it for a fact. If he's

comin' here for grub he can have it. If it's information he's lookin' for he won't get it."

Tascosa tossed some brush on the fire. As it flamed up, the sheriff and his men forded the river and walked their jaded horses into the circle of firelight.

"Hi, boys," Beaudry greeted them with a wave of his pudgy hand. He was a lantern-jawed individual with a wisp of black mustache that failed to hide his cruel mouth. "Smelled your fire a ways back. Didn't know who we'd find here."

Tascosa stepped forward.

"Maverick will shuffle up some grub for yuh if yuh'll light," he said.

"No time for that tonight, Tascosa," Beaudry returned. "Much obliged just the same. Where you from?"

"Down to the Kiowa country. Jest pulled in here about sundown. Came up by way of the old trail after leaving the North Fork."

"Humph," the sheriff murmured. It was impossible to say whether he was pleased or not. "See anyone?"

"Nary a soul . . . I take it you're lookin' for certain parties."

"Yeh," Beaudry laughed with a preoccupied air. "Been out all day on a red hot tip that some of the wild bunch has come out of the Strip with somethin' on their minds."

"Well, you ought to know where to look for them, if anybody does," Little Bill volunteered. The tone with which it was uttered made it anything but the compliment the words in themselves might have conveyed. As it was, every man present caught the sinister import of the remark. To make it more pointed, Link Appling chuckled brazenly.

The sheriff's mouth twisted into a mirthless grin and he fixed his eyes on Little Bill.

"I don't know whether I get you or not, Bill," he muttered tonelessly, "unless you mean that I been the sheriff of this county long enough to know my way around."

"What else could I mean, Cash?" the red-haired one inquired with a bland smile.

Beaudry could have slain him for his cool impudence. But he had been given a way out and he decided to take it.

"Oh, nothin' at all, I reckon," he grumbled. "I'm just a little touchy about the way things have been breakin' against me of late. I figure to have better luck tonight. We'll cut across as far as the railroad."

"Your broncs won't take you far," said Tascosa. "They're leg weary."

"That's why I'm here," Beaudry declared. "I'm commandeerin' your horses."

"Wait a minute!" Little Bill whipped out fiercely. "Let me get this right. Do you mean you're ridin' in here and takin' our horses whether we'll have it or not?"

"That's the idea," Beaudry answered bluntly. "The law gives me the right to take 'em, and that's what I'm doin'. We won't have no argument about that. You can pick 'em up in Bowie tomorrow."

"But our ponies have been on the go all day," Tascosa argued. His eyes were hard. He was not overly solicitous about the horses, but he knew trouble could not be avoided if the sheriff insisted on taking Little Bill's horse.

"You ain't been pushin' 'em by the looks of 'em," said Beaudry. "That claybank there is as bright as a dollar. Whose horse is it?"

"He's my horse," Little Bill informed him, "and you ain't takin' him—law or no law!" His eyes were smoking with indignation.

"I'm sorry to have to go contrary to your wishes," said Beaudry patronizingly, "but he appears to be the best in the bunch, and I'm takin' him." He turned to his men. "Get the saddles off these nags, boys; we've been here too long already. I'll take the big horse."

"Better not try it," Little Bill warned. "Put a hand on him and I'm throwin' a gun on you, sheriff or whatever you are!"

Beaudry did not back down. It was too late for that.

"You better use your head," he blazed as he slipped out of his saddle. "Start a gun-play here and I'll finish it!"

Luther edged over to his brother's side.

"Bill, let this thing drop," he urged. "We don't want no trouble with this man. He'll slap you into jail and be glad of the chance."

"Keep out of this!" Bill flung back. "I'm handlin' it, Luther."

"You mean you're makin' a damned fine mess of things," said Luther. "I tell you it's gone far enough." Without warning he poked a .45 in his brother's side. "Now you stand still," he ordered. "I'm takin' your guns."

Chapter III

THE blood drained away from Little Bill's cheeks as he stood without moving even his eyes. Luther's attention was riveted on him. They were brothers, but for the moment that had exactly no importance at all. The others watched breathlessly. Tascosa and the Sawbuck men had no thought of interfering; Luther had made his play, and he would have to see it through; but to a man, they expected to see Little Bill suddenly spring into the air and come down with his guns popping. The advantage would be all with Luther, and it was in the rules of the game that he would do something about it.

To their amazement, however, Little Bill half-raised his hands.

"All right, Luther," he said. "I guess it'll have to be your way." He spoke without anger.

"I'm right glad you had a flash of sense," his brother drawled. He took possession of Little Bill's guns and turned them over to Tascosa. The old man's hands trembled slightly as he took them.

Beaudry was relieved too.

"Much obliged to you, Luther." He grinned in a vain attempt to hide his agitation. "Bill will thank you too when he gets a chance to think things over. It's all right to be hot-headed, but there's no use lettin' a little misunderstandin' make a fool of yuh. Now———"

"Beaudry—it's the horses you want, ain't it?" Luther cut him off sharply. "Well, there they are. You get your saddles on 'em and be on your way. Nobody here is interested in hearing you exercise your jaw. You're overdue to leave right now."

Cash bristled wrathfully at this fresh affront.

"That's more than plenty out of you," he sneered. "I aim to remember a few things that happened here tonight."

"You won't be the only one," Little Bill muttered cryptically.

The few minutes of darkness following the long twilight were giving way to the silvery radiance of the moon. In the short while it took Beaudry and his deputies to saddle the commandeered horses it grew appreciably lighter, until it was possible to see distinctly for long distances. The sheriff had some trouble mounting the gelding. He got up at last. His men were already in their saddles.

"See you in Bowie tomorrow!" he called to Tascosa.

"Yeh, and you see that them horses is returned as is!" the old man shouted back.

The little cavalcade began to move down the valley, setting a course well out from the black smudge of trees that lined the river bottom. Tascosa and his men gathered about the wagon and stared after them.

"A lot of hell to raise over a horse," the old man grumbled. "I told you them claybanks is bad luck, Bill."

"Bad luck for some people, you mean," the red-haired one answered, his tone ominous. "I'll thank you for my guns now."

Tascosa handed them over.

"We ain't seen the end of this," he said. "He'll make us plenty trouble from now on."

"I figure that's true," Little Bill admitted. "I hate to get a man in a jam on my account, but I couldn't help it this once. If I thought anythin' was to be gained by walkin' wide of him now I'd let him get away with his play; but I know better. I said no man was takin' Six-gun. I meant it, and I mean it now. Luther stopped me once. Don't none of you-all try it a second time. I'm warnin' you I'm on my own. I've got an ace up my sleeve and I'm playin' it!"

As they gazed at him, wondering just what he meant, they saw him put his fingers to his mouth. A long-drawn, piercing whistle rang out. It carried down the river to the little group of horsemen, by now upwards of two hundred yards away. It bore instant result, for Six-gun reared up on its hind legs and pawed the air wildly. Beaudry was hard put to stay in his saddle. Little Bill whistled again, and the horse rose until it seemed it must topple over on its back.

"There goes Beaudry!" Link cried. "Six-gun has thrown him off! Boy, look at that horse! He'll kill that fool if he don't let go of the bridle rein!"

It was true. The big gelding seemed intent on pawing the life out of the man on the ground. Beaudry's companions seemed not to know what to do. Little Bill whistled a third time.

"That fetched him!" Scotty exclaimed excitedly. "Mr. Sheriff has let go!"

Six-gun had whirled around and was racing back to the wagon now, its mane and tail flattened out. Suddenly a gun barked. Beaudry, beside himself with rage, had fired from where he lay.

"Damn him, ain't that a skunk for yuh!" Little Bill cried, expecting to see the horse go down.

But the gelding came on with unabated speed. Little Bill ran to the wagon. It took him only a second to get his rifle out of his bedroll and fill his shirt with cartridges.

"You, Six-gun!" he shouted as the trembling horse dashed in among them. The animal trotted over to him. The sheriff and his posse were returning; Cash riding double.

"Bill, what are you goin' to do?" It was Luther. His voice was a hoarse croak.

For answer, Little Bill threw his gun to his shoulder and began to pump it. The posse pulled up short. If none of them pitched out of their saddles it was only because he was purposely shooting low.

"Luther, jerk that saddle off and put mine on!" he whipped out. "I'll hold 'em off!"

"You're makin' a mistake!" his brother cried.

"It's me that's makin' it! Did that skunk mark Six-gun?"

"Just burned him a little on the right leg."

Tascosa and the others would have rushed up, but Little Bill warned them back.

"No need of you gettin' mixed up in this," he said. "It's my funeral—if it is a funeral!"

He blazed away in the direction of the posse again.

"There's your horse," Luther told him a moment later. "You wait a minute and I'll go with you."

"You're stayin' right here," Bill insisted. "You tell Beaudry if he comes after me to come a smokin'; I ain't shootin' to miss from now on."

He sailed into his saddle without effort and raced away. A few minutes later the sound of water being lashed into spray told them he was crossing the Cimarron.

Beaudry and his deputies dashed after him, emptying their guns as they rode. Once across the river, however, they pulled up in a hurry, for well up the slope, Little Bill's rifle had begun to flash. The little puffs of dust that his slugs kicked up were dangerously close, proving that he was quickly getting the range.

Tascosa and the others saw the posse confer briefly, and after sending a futile volley up the slope, jog back to the wagon. Beaudry soon had the air blue with his cursing.

"Damn his hide, I'll make one horrible example of him!" he thundered. "I can't waste no time on him to-night, but I'll sure fetch him for this!"

"I wouldn't take on too much about it," Tascosa counseled. "He had a lot on his side, Cash. The horse is the apple of his eye. We had another bronc here that you could have had without any fuss."

"And you call that an excuse for defyin' the law?" The sheriff's face was purple with wrath.

"I won't call it an excuse," Tascosa drawled with provoking deliberation, "but there's often what is known as extenuatin' circumstances. For one thing, your reputation with a horse ain't of the best—and you more'n lived up to it tonight. I can stand for most anythin', but it kinda rubs me the wrong way to see a man use a gun on horseflesh. This majesty of the law that seems to be troublin' you so much don't cover anythin' like that."

"Is that so?" Cash ground out contemptuously. "You sound to me like you're lookin' for trouble. Maybe I can make you a little."

"Well, suppose you do then!" old Tas flared back, suddenly angry. "I ain't askin' no favors of you. Jest be sure if you start somethin' that there'll be a showdown 'fore I git through. Now if you've got any outlaws to look up tonight you better take Scotty's pony and be on your way."

Breathing vengeance, Beaudry led his posse away. For an hour and more after they had gone, Tascosa and the others conversed in low tones about the fire, now burned down to a few coals. All were of the opinion that it would be the part of wisdom for Little Bill to avoid Bowie for the present.

"But I'm afraid he won't listen to that," said Luther. "You know how he feels about Doc Southard's girl. He ain't seen her in over two months, and he's got his heart set on it. I don't know whether it's him or Paint Johnson who's got the inside track with Martha. But it don't matter; you know how Bill is when he gits any-thin' into his head."

"Wal, Paint's just a kid yet, but he's a mighty nice boy," Tascosa declared weightily. "If Bill's worryin' at all about him he better stay out of Bowie until this thing blows over. He won't be beatin' anybody's time if he gits hisself tossed into jail. Mebbe you'd best take one of these broncs they left us and see if you can't locate the little varmint. He'll be safe here at the wagon tonight."

It didn't take Luther long to find his brother.

"So there you are, eh?" old Tas called out banter-ingly as the two rode up. "You sure gave quite an ac-count of yourself, Bill."

"Yeh, I was sure shootin' at them there for a min-ute," the red-haired one grinned sheepishly. "I told him he couldn't have my horse and I kept my word. I wasn't takin' no chance of havin' him show up tomor-row with a story that the geldin' had been shot out from under him or that the Sontags had lifted him. I'd likely never have seen Six-gun again. Beaudry would give me an order against the county for fifty dollars, and I could like it or leave it."

"Nobody is sayin' you didn't have your way, you little fightin' runt," Maverick Williams remarked. "Now all you got to do is pay for it."

"I don't mind payin' for value received," said Little Bill, "but I ain't givin' myself up until I know what the charge is."

"Then you agree you shouldn't go into Bowie tomorrow?" Tascosa asked with frank surprise.

"I admit I shouldn't, but I'm goin' just the same."

"Why be a fool, Bill?" the old man demanded heatedly.

"I can't help it; I got to go. I've been countin' on it for weeks. I'll ride in early in the mornin' and stay just a few minutes. With any luck at all I'll be on my way before Beaudry gets back."

"Where'll you go then?" asked Luther.

"I'll head for the Panhandle. You'll be down next month. I'll meet up with you all right."

"Be a lot better if you started back right now," Tascosa insisted. "I could get the lay of things for you and send word down by somebody. But I ain't goin' to argue," he added as Little Bill would have interrupted. "I know there's no chance of changin' your mind. You're as stubborn as your old man. I could see him in everythin' you did tonight. The old fightin' fool—" Tascosa shook his head at some ancient memory of Waco Stillings and himself. "When his joints got so full of rheumatiz he couldn't fork a horse no more he gits himself a job as a express messenger so he can keep on packin' a gun on his hip! You aimin' to see your father tomorrow, Bill?"

"I will if he's in from his run. He may not be on tonight."

"I'm hopin' he ain't," Luther remarked moodily.

"Why do you say that?" his brother asked.

"Just a hunch maybe." Luther tossed away his cigarette and watched it die out in the grass. "That bunch on the Skull, movin' east, and Beaudry's talk about goin' as far as the railroad sounds to me like the Rock Island's night express might run into some trouble."

"Pop knows how to take care of himself," Little Bill declared.

"That's just the trouble; he won't give up as long as he can raise a gun. He thinks he's as good as ever. We know better. It ain't no trick to fade him now."

For some reason, Little Bill's mood was as sombre as his brother's. The others felt it.

"Aw shucks," Link chided them, "why borrow trouble? There's ten banks hoisted to every train that's stuck up."

"And jest because it's ten times as easy," Tascosa declared with a chuckle. "I didn't figger when I mentioned Waco's name that it would bring on anything like this. I was afraid he might go gunnin' for the sheriff when he heard about tonight." He got to his feet and stretched preparatory to rolling up in his blanket. "I'll see him tomorrow, Bill, and tell him what's what. You better roll in now."

Little Bill looked after his horse before he turned in. By the time he had washed out the crease Beaudry's bullet had made and smeared it with axle-grease, the camp was asleep. He got his bedroll then and stretched out beside the wagon. The train of thought Luther had started was still with him and he could not throw it off. He recalled Tascosa's words about a claybank being unlucky.

"Can't be anythin' to that," he brooded. "Pop's never even seen the horse."

When sleep came finally it brought dreams of a train rushing through the night; of the ghostly shrieking of a locomotive's whistle; of an old, spindle-shanked man dozing in his chair in an express-car.

Chapter IV

THE heavy, combination mail-and-express car began to roll and lurch on its trucks as the train gathered speed. Number Nine was running eighteen minutes late to-night. Coming out of Medora, Quinlan, the engineer, began to open her up in earnest. He had fifty-five miles of nearly straight track ahead, with only a stop for water at Skull Creek and the bare possibility of being flagged at Wetona between him and the end of his run at Bowie. He expected to pick up at least twelve of those eighteen minutes.

The glow from the open fire-box played redly over big Ike Bonura, his fireman, and the sweat that dripped from Ike's streaming brow as he toiled with his shovel fell like drops of blood. He had been building steam for half-an-hour. As he continued to pile it on, the cinders fell in an angry shower on the roof of the mail and express car next the tender.

Dick Ferris, the railway mail clerk, braced himself as he distributed the stuff that had come aboard at Medora. He was a colorless, thin-faced man; the green eye-shade that he wore cast a sickly tinge over his countenance.

"This rattler seems to be going places, Waco!" he exclaimed, addressing the old, hatchet-faced man, three times his age, who rode express with him. "They must have been doing some work on the roadbed along here. We seem to be kicking up a lot of dust." He cast an eye at the ventilators in the roof of the car. "I hope we don't hit a loose rail."

"Say, you're right cheerful tonight, ain't yuh?" Waco returned. He was sprawled out comfortably in an old side-arm chair. Without removing his thin shanks from the steel express box on which they were propped he half-turned to send an inquiring glance at Ferris. "What seems to be eatin' yuh? Yuh been carryin' on that-a-way all evenin'."

His resemblance to his sons was marked. He was taller than Little Bill, but their faces had been carved from the same mold. There was a quizzical expression in their eyes that was identical.

"Nothing eating me," Ferris answered, "but I'll be glad when we roll into Bowie."

"What yuh kickin' about then?" Waco demanded. "We're certainly rollin'."

"Yeah—but a lot can happen in fifty miles. You're not fooling me by pretending not to have anything on your mind. I know you've got something in the safe. You didn't have your hand off your gun as we stood in Medora."

"Well, it's a purty rough, tough sort of a town," Waco laughed.

"Yeah—so tough you couldn't get the door locked quick enough."

Waco scratched his head reflectively. His closely cropped red hair was still as thick as his sons'.

"I didn't know you was so observin', Dick," he mused aloud. "I don't mind admittin' we got a little stuff aboard tonight. I reckon it's safe enough now; we ain't openin' up for nothin' this side of Bowie."

"I hope you're right," Ferris murmured nervously. "I'm still carrying one of the slugs in my leg that I got over at Waukomis last spring. I don't want any more of that."

He began to make up the pouch for Bowie. A mournful blast of the whistle split the night air. It sucked in through the ventilators with a blood-chilling whine. Ferris' head went up with a jerk.

"Jest blowin' for the Santee bridge," Waco explained hurriedly. He was surprised to find his own throat dry.

They roared across the bridge a moment later with unabated speed. Ferris went on with his work. Waco had nothing to occupy him but his thoughts.

As a rule, they kept up a running fire of conversation. Tonight, however, they found less and less to say to each other as Number Nine rolled up the miles. In some peculiar way the air had become charged with an electric tension.

Ferris accepted it with pathetic resignation. His pale face was pasty-looking, his hair damp across his forehead. Waco tried to throw it off. His nerves had never bothered him, and he told himself there was no reason for them to snarl tonight. And yet, when he felt the train lose speed and an almost imperceptible tightening of the air hose as the engineer prepared to slap on the brakes, he felt a cold chill race down his spine.

The two men found themselves staring at each other and saying nothing. It was only a moment before the pressure was removed from the airline. The wheels began to click faster again.

Waco grinned a little foolishly at Ferris. Both now realized that the momentary loss of speed meant that they were rushing past Ardusa, their flag stop. Quinlan had only slowed down to see if the light was against him.

It was Ferris' turn to laugh off key now.

"What's the matter, Waco?" he prodded. "What pulled you out of your chair?"

"Nothin' but your damn nonsense!" the old man snapped. "You got me seein' things too! You get the board out and we'll play a hand or two of seven-up. Anythin' would be better than sittin' around like this, waitin' for somethin' to happen."

After the first hand or two the game became just a perfunctory business of shuffling and laying down pieces of pasteboard, for their minds were not on what they were doing. Both were listening, tense and alert, to every sound and movement of the train. Thirty minutes of it was all they could stand. Ferris had just caught himself dealing poker instead of seven-up.

"That's more than enough," he scolded. He glanced at his watch. "10:52, Waco."

"Yeh. Ought to be slowin' down for the Skull Creek tank directly."

"Damned lonely spot."

"Yeh—" Waco answered laconically.

Presently Quinlan began to use the air. The sharp

clicking of the wheels died away to a dull rattle. Panting lustily, Number Nine's big iron horse slid up to the Skull Creek tank.

The sharp hiss of steam from the exhaust valves and the whine of escaping air reached Waco and Ferris. The night was still, save for the droning of the cicadas. They heard the fireman climb over the coal; the lowering of the spout; the rush of water into the tender.

These were all familiar, reassuring sounds. Ferris mopped his face in relief.

"Guess it's all right," he grinned. "If we get by here———"

His words were lost in the sharp, staccato crash of half-a-dozen guns, the slugs pinging off the steel tender or plowing into the walls of the wooden express car.

Hoarse cries followed. Men could be heard running alongside the train. Up ahead there was another burst of gunfire.

Waco and Ferris had leaped to their feet.

"They're here!" Ferris gasped. "I knew it! I felt it in my bones tonight!"

"Jest keep your pants on," Waco ground out harshly. "There's a bunch of 'em out there!"

A wire grille separated the railway post-office from the rest of the car. Ferris drew his gun as he retreated behind it.

"Better put that gun out of sight," Waco advised. "It'll be just like committin' suicide if they catch you with it."

"You mean you're going to let them in?" Ferris cried.

"I may have to do that. I don't intend to be foolish about this. . . . Follow my lead and you'll be all right."

"If they come at me, I'm shooting!" Ferris said stubbornly.

"Have it your way," Waco muttered. "If you use that shootin'-iron you better shoot to kill. But it ain't you they're after. There's been a leak somehow; they know I got twenty thousand in currency in the safe. Well, they ain't got it yet, I can tell 'em!"

Almost immediately there came a loud banging on the door.

"Come on, open up in there!" a hoarse voice bellowed. "I've got dynamite enough here to blow this car to hell if you don't move lively."

Waco took his gun from the holster and tossed it on his desk. His nerves were not troubling him now. An old, lean gray wolf stalking its prey could not have been cooler or more deliberate than he as he dropped to his knees and spun the combination dial of the safe.

From without came a second summons to open the door.

"Who are you?" Waco demanded this time.

"You know who we are, Waco!" an angry voice shouted back. "You quit your nonsense and git that door open!"

Waco recognized the speaker. It was Smoke Sontag.

"Is that you Smoke?" he stalled as he took a package from the safe and dropped it into the little cast-iron stove—unused for weeks—which stood in the corner of the car.

"You damn well know it is!" the outlaw answered.

"All right, I'll open up," the old man promised.

This was robbery on a rather unique plane, in that both parties were known to the other. Here was no case of bandits attacking behind a handkerchief or a black mask. Like the Daltons and the Doolins, the Sontag gang had a name for ruthlessness that was well-calculated to strike fear whenever it appeared, and they made the most of it.

Waco was searching for a package with which to replace the one he had taken from the safe. He found one—similar in size and weight—a package of billheads, from a Medora printer, on their way to Bowie. It was the work of a moment to deface the label and toss the package into the safe.

He gave the dial a spin and hurried to the door, flashing a glance at Ferris as he fumbled with the lock.

"Git your hands up when they come in—and keep your lip buttoned!" he cautioned him.

The heavy door was run back with a bang, due to assistance from without.

Three of the Sontags climbed into the car. Smoke did the talking. He was a giant in size, fear-proof, reckless and a born leader of men.

"Come on get 'em up higher!" he barked at Waco. The old man raised his hands above his head. "That's right, just keep reachin' for the stars. I ain't takin' no chance on you." He spoke to his brother. "You take care of the mail clerk, Grat: Shorty and me'll 'tend to Waco."

Grat Sontag, a weasel-eyed, pockmarked killer, already had Ferris backed into a corner. The mail clerk didn't move fast enough for him, however, and Grat grazed his head with a bullet.

It was neat shooting, but Ferris thought the miss was accidental; that he was to be slain even though he had his hands in the air. Foolishly he reached for the gun he had hidden. Grat did not miss this time. With a tired sigh, the clerk crumpled up on the floor.

Smoke ignored the interruption.

"Waco—you got twenty thousand in currency with you tonight. Where is it?"

"In the safe." Waco Stillings' eyes were cold and stony.

"See if he's got a gun on him," Smoke ordered.

Grat ran his hands over Waco and found nothing.

"All right, take your hands down, and open up that safe!"

"Smoke, it'll mean my job if I open up that safe for yuh," the old man declared solemnly.

"It'll mean your funeral if you don't!" Grat Sontag whipped out viciously. He poked a gun at Waco. "Get her open!"

Waco whirled on him indignantly.

"Say, don't you git so reckless with your gun-talk!" he blazed. "I ain't no scared mail clerk. I'll open this safe, but I'll take my time about it; and I'm remindin' yuh to think twice before yuh shoot me down like yuh did Ferris there. If anythin' happens to me my boys will see that I git justice if they have to chase yuh to hell to git it!"

Smoke waved Grat back. Both had some acquaintance with the Stillings boys.

"That's all right, Waco," Grat grumbled, "just open her up; we won't have no trouble with you."

"All right, jest so we understand each other," the old man muttered as he bent over the safe. "I don't mind a little gun-play now and then. I've shot it out with better men than the best of yuh—and they always had a chance to fill their hand before I cut down on 'em. Less than that is jest murder, and I don't mind tellin' yuh so to your teeth."

"Suppose you tighten your lip a little!" Grat jerked out. "We ain't got all night to wait here. Get her open!"

"She's open," Waco announced.

"Then get your hands up and back away!" Smoke barked at him.

He kept Waco covered as Grat rifled the safe. Shorty Pierce, the third man, scooped up the gun that Waco had tossed on the desk. It took only a second or two. Waco was watching them craftily. Grat did not bother to examine the package he had taken from the safe.

"Come on, Shorty!" Smoke commanded. "You and Grat pile out of here; I'll follow."

The two men ran to the door and jumped to the ground. Smoke backed away after them.

"Don't show your face until after we ride away," he warned. "You'll sure get busted if you do."

"Go ahead; I ain't stoppin' yuh," Waco flung back at him fiercely.

A minute later, after firing an admonitory fusillade that rattled harmlessly against the side of the express car, the Sontags rode away. Members of the train crew who had found discretion the better part of valor ran up now. The conductor peered into the express car to find Waco bent down over Ferris' lifeless body. He started to climb in.

"Good God, don't waste any time askin' questions!" Waco snarled at him. "Give Jerry the highball and git this train rollin'!"

"But Ferris looks as though he was badly wounded," the conductor protested. "If there is a doctor aboard we ought to get him up here."

"No doctor is goin' to help this boy," Waco told him. "He's dead. He's likely not to be the only one if we don't pull out of here before Smoke discovers that he didn't get what he came for."

"What do you mean by that?" Richards, the conductor, asked.

"I mean the money is there in the stove," said Waco. "All the Sontags got was some printed matter—and Smoke's sense of humor ain't up to appreciatin' anythin' like that."

Chapter V

It was less than sixteen miles from the scene of the holdup to Bowie, for the Skull flowed to the northeast for some distance before it joined the Cimarron. Number Nine made the run in record time. Five minutes after she pulled into the Bowie yards news that the Sontags had boarded her in spectacular fashion, killing a mail clerk but failing to get the money they were after, through the coolheadedness of Waco Stillings, was winging its way over town.

A crowd gathered at the station and saw Ferris' body removed from the train. Telegraph wires had begun to hum. From Oklahoma City came word that Heck Short, U. S. Marshal, and his man-hunters were leaving for Bowie at once. From even more distant Kansas City came a message authorizing a reward for the capture of Ferris' slayers, dead or alive. Newspapers asked for details of the holdup.

Waco found it a little bewildering as he sat in the division superintendent's office. He had been enjoined against saying anything until the Marshal arrived. A stricture of that nature was akin to locking the barn after the horse has been stolen, for alleged eye-witnesses among the passengers had ostensibly purveyed all details already.

Some time after midnight Waco made his way up-town. He lived beyond the business section. It was his intention to go directly home, but he had no more than set foot on the main street than he was hailed right and left. Lights still burned brightly in Bowie's saloons, for the town retained enough of its frontier character to refuse to be put to bed until it was good and ready to go. As a result, Waco's progress became something of a triumphant procession. Various refreshments were urged on him, but he refused them successfully until he reached the Longhorn Saloon. There Sam Swift, Bowie's new mayor, captured him and propelled him inside.

"Here he is, boys!" Sam beamed as he pushed Waco up to the bar. "He put Bowie on the map tonight! The drinks is on me!"

The crowd cheered. Waco was embarrassed. He had never found himself a hero before. In the past he had often been in the public eye in Bowie, but that was on those occasions when it used to delight him to ride into town with a bunch of punchers and express his exuberance by shooting out the lights.

When Waco refused to enlarge on the story of what had happened at Skull Creek crossing, they put it down to modesty. It didn't make any difference really; they had heard enough to give them a pretty definite idea of what had occurred.

Some one else bought a drink, and then another and another. Sam had his arm around Waco now.

"He's an old fightin' son-of-a-gun, boys!" he bellowed. "A little starched in the legs, but he's the man who ought to be the next sheriff of this county!"

The crowd shouted its approval.

"Speakin' of the sheriff," Sam continued with mock concern, "has some body mislaid him? Where *is* Beaudry?"

"He's right here, Sam," Cash answered for himself from the door. He slapped the dust off his shoulders as he strode in with his chief deputy. He was panting a little breathlessly. "Let me up to the bar; I sure crave a drink."

He filled a glass to the brim and dashed the contents off deftly. The crowd was watching him, its attitude a mixture of indifference and hostility.

"That tip you had was certainly red hot, just as you said," Sam Swift volunteered. "Suppose you've heard the news."

"I didn't only hear it, but if I'd had some fresh horses I would have been right in it," Beaudry enlightened them. "We covered some country since mornin'. Our broncs was staggerin' when we ran into Tas Cummings' outfit camped at Cherokee crossing on the Cimarron. I commandeered their horses, but they wa'n't none too fresh after comin' up all the way from the North Fork. We kept on down the river until we came to the Skull. We'd just turned up the creek when we heard shootin'. . . . I knew what it meant."

"You must have missed them by just a few minutes," Sam suggested. His tone was solicitous to the point of being mocking. Beaudry failed to catch it.

"I'd had Smoke dead to rights tonight," he ground out savagely. "I didn't intend to waste no time tryin' to take that bunch alive. It was just the damnedest luck a man ever had that I missed 'em. We came on, best we could, but the train had pulled out before we got there." He shook his head to express his bitterness. "Wa'n't no point in tryin' to overhaul Smoke's bunch with the stuff we was ridin'."

"Guess you was doin' well to get back to Bowie," Sam declared solemnly.

"Just about crawled in," Cash agreed. "But I'm promisin' you I ain't done!" he burst out with a sudden show of spirit. "This thing's personal between Smoke and me now! I'll fetch him!" He banged the bar with his fist to emphasize his words.

"Luck can't be against us always," Blackie Chilton, his chief deputy, declared.

"That's what I say, Blackie!" There was a calculating light in Beaudry's eyes as he glanced furtively up and down the bar. He was intent on ascertaining what sort of an impression he had made. An interruption from the end of the bar did not add to his pleasure.

"Why don't you deputize Waco?" a raucous voice demanded.

"Say, that's no joke!" the sheriff reprimanded the speaker. "I don't yield to no man in my respect for what he did tonight!" He forced his way up to the old man. "I certainly want to shake your hand, Waco," he declared humbly. "I never heard of a gamer thing—standin' up in front of a gang of recognized killers and doin' what you did! I'm mighty proud of yuh."

Waco let him pump his hand. He liked Beaudry as little as did his sons.

"I'm buyin' for the crowd now!" Cash boomed. "I want you to drink with me to Waco!" He had said nothing about his difficulty with Little Bill. He felt the time was hardly propitious for mentioning it. "Well, here's to you!" he exclaimed as he raised his glass.

" 'Bout time you made a speech, Waco," Sam Swift urged. The crowd took it up, but Waco refused to warm to the idea.

"His modesty is right becomin'!" Cash laughed. He slapped Waco on the back familiarly. "I bet Smoke Sontag is livin' up to his name right now. Can you imagine him, boys, when he found that all he'd got was a bunch of Otto Hahn's Purity Market billheads? I bet his eyes popped!"

It won a laugh from the crowd. As for Waco, his eyes seemed about to pop too. Cash had just recalled a fact that had escaped him until now. It was nothing less than that the label he had so hurriedly destroyed before tossing the package of billheads into the safe was addressed to Otto Hahn, the local butcher. Having forgotten it, he could not have spoken about it to anyone. How, then, did Cash Beaudry come by his information?

It suddenly dawned on Waco that Blackie Chilton, the deputy, was regarding him narrowly. Blackie had caught the slip. Too late the old man tried to cover up with a dissembling grin. Waco could have kicked himself for his carelessness.

"I'm goin' along now," he said presently. "Chalk will have supper waitin' for me."

"All right, Waco," Beaudry exclaimed. "See you at the inquest in the mornin'."

With his hair pulling a little from the four or five drinks he had imbibed, Waco continued on home. A light burned in the kitchen of the little house he occupied. Little Bill and Luther called it home when they were in town. The real head of the establishment, however, was not Waco nor his sons, but Chalk Whipple, a scolding old tyrant who did the cooking and looked after things in general, and who would have risked his life at a moment's notice for any one of them.

Like Waco and old Tascosa, Chalk had been a cowboy in his younger days. Years back, he had lost his left leg in a railroad smash-up while on his way to Kansas City with a train-load of beef. He had been stamping around on a wooden substitute ever since and bossing Waco and the boys and managing to keep the little house spotless. He flung open the door now before Waco reached it.

"Here at last, eh?" he scolded. "You can't keep things hot forever."

"Quit snappin' now," Waco protested. "This is a kinda unusual night."

"I know; I heard the news," Chalk retorted as he

turned to the stove. "I suppose you're a hero now. You look out that you ain't a dead one before the week is out."

"Yeh, I been thinkin' of that," Waco sighed as he lowered himself into a chair. "I reckon the Sontags will be out to git me for sure now."

"If you don't know it you're crazy!" Chalk glared at him. He put a platter of ham and eggs on the table and poured out the coffee, with a cup for himself. "Why didn't you let 'em have the money? You didn't stand to lose nothin'."

"Not so fast there," Waco argued as he picked up knife and fork. "I figger I had plenty to lose. It was my duty to stay with that money as long as I could. I've made it a rule with myself, and I tried to hammer it into the boys too, that when you pass your word— stick to it."

He ate a mouthful or two.

"Bill and Luther will be here in the mornin'," he told Chalk. "Beaudry saw 'em on the Cimarron this evenin'."

"I bet they'll have somethin' to say about this." Chalk shook his head thoughtfully. "I bet they agree with me that you hadn't ought to done what you did."

"Mebbe. When I saw Grat Sontag shoot that boy down without givin' him a chance I made up my mind that they wouldn't get that money unless they killed me too."

"That's what they'll try now. They'll be layin' for yuh."

"If that's the case, I better try to get them before

they get me. I ain't exactly on the shelf yet. I'm packin' my old guns from now on."

The talk turned to Beaudry.

"What do you figger he was doin' down there?" Chalk asked.

"I reckon he was coverin' their stand and get-away —if you want it straight from the shoulder," said Waco. "He says he was tipped off that the Sontags was out of the Strip, but he don't say how he got the tip. I don't know why he should have been anywhere near the Skull crossing tonight lookin' for outlaws unless he knew we was goin' to be stuck up."

"You bet he knew," Chalk declared emphatically. "Beaudry and his possemen and the Sontags is one outfit if you ask me. Him bein' sheriff, he hears things. How do you know it wa'n't Beaudry that learned the money was comin' through tonight?"

"Most likely it was," Waco agreed as he sat down his empty cup. "He was spreadin' himself down the street a few minutes ago. Gave himself dead away."

"Yeh? How do you figger that?"

Waco had been on the point of confiding fully in Chalk, but he thought better of it now; Chalk often went downtown in the evening and talked too much if he had a few drinks in him.

"Oh, just by all of his talk," he answered vaguely. "It was too loose for me. Heck Short will be here in the mornin' to take charge of things."

"He's a good man," said Chalk. "Chances are he may start somethin'."

"I reckon so," Waco murmured, and to himself he

added, "and finish it too when he hears what I've got to say. Cash sure talked himself into an awful hole tonight."

Across town in Beaudry's little office Blackie Chilton was echoing that very thought to Cash.

"I tell you old Waco got it!" he growled. "I could see it on his face! It was a damn fool crack to make!"

"You've said that before," Beaudry snarled back. "I know it was a damn bad slip. I shouldn't have opened my mouth until I found out what he had been sayin'. But don't keep throwin' it into me. I ain't worryin' about that old juniper."

"You're dumber than I thought you were if you think that," Chilton rifled at him. "That old bird is poison if I know anythin'. You do a lot of chin waggin', but I'd like to hear you explain how you knew them billheads was in the package and had that Dutchman's name on 'em."

"Maybe I won't have to do much explainin'," Cash grumbled. "If I forget what happened on the river this evenin' Waco will listen to reason. It'll get down to keepin' Little Bill out of the jug, and that will interest the old man."

"I'll be everlastin'ly damned!" Blackie exploded. "On the level, Cash, you're so thick I can't figger why Smoke ever bothered with yuh. What difference does it make whether Waco Stillings forgets what you said or not? Didn't two dozen men hear it? Have yuh got any idea Heck Short won't have it repeated to him?

If that's your idea of coverin' us, I'm pullin' out of this town tonight."

"There's nothin' to stop Waco from sayin' he told somebody what was in the package, is there?"

"And yuh got the story from that certain party, eh?" Chilton sneered. "I'm tellin' yuh that's a lot of nonsense—even if yuh got the old man to play along with yuh. Who was that unknown party who heard all this talk that he told you? That's what Short will want to know. He'll run it down; I know him. He'll have you so mixed before noon tomorrow that you'll wish you had wings to git you out of Bowie."

"There's another way of doin' it," Cash muttered darkly.

"Yeh, and that's the way you better take. Just be sure you git him. Ever'body'll say it was Smoke who done it."

Beaudry's flabby face was damp with perspiration. He and Chilton had been wrangling for half an hour. The penalty for the slip he had made was not confined to his fear that he might presently find himself afoul of the law; there was Smoke Sontag's displeasure to be reckoned with, for as the sheriff of Cimarron county he was important to the gang, and anything that interfered with that arrangement would not be overlooked. It hurried him to a decision.

"All right," he wheezed, his eyes steeling. "He had this comin' to him. He always walks over to the tracks just after daylight to get the Kansas City papers they throw off to him from the California Limited."

"Yeh, follows that old drywash," Chilton monotoned. "Kinda lonely there; nobody around at all."

Beaudry swallowed heavily.

"I'll be waitin' for him tomorrow mornin'."

Chapter VI

Since boyhood Waco had rolled out of his blankets at sun up. It followed that he was astir early the following morning. He had a pardonable interest in seeing the papers this day, a fact that he was at some pains to conceal, and he even lingered to build the fire before starting off across the flats to the tracks. He had only a quarter of a mile to go.

The haze of early morning was beginning to rise as he stepped out of the kitchen door. He had strapped on his old gun-belt with its pair of long-barrelled .44's. Settling it about his hips, he strode off. It felt good to feel the old guns slapping against his legs once more. Unconsciously his grizzled face wrinkled into a grin.

The Limited rolled out of the Bowie yards while he was yet within a short distance of the house. A low toot of the whistle told him that Ed Myers, the engineer, had tossed off his papers.

He felt free to quicken his step now and he was soon swinging along. Lulled to carelessness by the familiarity of the scene, he had no thought of danger. The path he was using brought him to the brink of the arroyo in a few minutes. It turned there and followed the wash. He made the turning but he took only a step or two when a gun roared from the opposite bank. The bullet struck him high enough in the shoulder to spin him around.

The suddenness of it had caught him all unprepared, but he had his guns out of the leather before the impact of the slug had swung him completely around. He knew what he faced now. His eyes drilled holes into the chaparral across the wash. It was not over twenty yards wide, but he could find no sign of the man who had fired at him.

Suddenly a gun barked at him a second time. The bullet carried his hat away. This time he caught a little puff of white smoke. With his guns only hip high he fired instantly at the spot. He took it for granted that he was facing one or more of the Sontags.

"They didn't wait long," he thought even as he glanced hurriedly about for cover of some sort. Finding none, he threw himself into the arroyo, rolling to the bottom.

His shoulder was bleeding freely. He was not worrying about that. He knew that unless he could get under the cut bank across the wash he was done for. Scrambling to his feet, he made a rush for it. Something warned him to throw himself flat on the ground just before he reached it. He was dropping when a gun cracked viciously on the bank above him. The bullet found its mark this time. He felt the slug burn through his lungs. Rolling over and over, he reached the overhung cut bank and propped himself up against it.

"Got me good that time," he gasped. His shirt was a bloody smear already. "This may be keno for me."

Something moved up on the bank. He fired at it with both guns.

"Come on and git me!" he taunted. "You got me down, damn yuh, but I'm still throwin' lead at yuh!"

He blazed away again and his fire was returned. He knew by now that he faced only one man. His assailant was becoming bolder. Waco understood why. Certainly the shooting was being heard in town. It couldn't be long before someone would be investigating the meaning of it.

The first shot fired had brought Chalk Whipple to the door. Waco's answering blast was explanation enough for Chalk.

"The Sontags are after him!" he screeched.

Beside his bed he kept an old U. S. Army carbine. Almost tearing the door from its hinges in his haste, he stamped into the house, grabbed the gun and a belt of cartridges and popped out again. In another second he was in full flight for the arroyo, his peg leg fairly flashing back and forth.

He was beyond the barn when a horseman rode into the yard and hailed him. Chalk recognized his voice and he spun around dizzily on his wooden leg to face him.

"Bill—is that you for a fact?" he cried.

"It ain't no one else, you old buzzard," Little Bill grinned. "What's all that shootin' goin' on down the arroyo?"

"It's your pa! The Sontags are after him, Bill!" Chalk shouted at him.

"The Sontags?" It didn't make sense. "What's the Sontags got to do with Pop?"

He caught the words "Rock Island," "stick up"— and "Waco tricked 'em so they didn't get a cent!"— in Chalk's excited explanation. He didn't wait for more. For the first time in his life he raked Six-gun with the spurs. The gelding leaped away as though shot out of a gun.

Chalk hopped along in his wake like a wounded fighting cock, cackling fiercely to himself, every bit as forbidding as he was grotesque.

From the arroyo came another exchange of shots. All was still then. Little Bill passed from sight only to reappear on the far bank a moment later, riding like a madman.

"Luther was right," he groaned, his eyes everywhere. "I only hope I'm in time!"

The bluejoint and patches of catclaw made a veritable thicket. A man on foot could crawl through it without being seen. Once he thought he saw the grass move. He fired instantly. Nothing happened.

"Just a breath of wind," he muttered glumly as he reached the spot and saw that the grass was not broken down. His blood began to run cold as he went on without drawing a shot. He knew he was a good target. The fact that no one banged away at him argued that whoever had jumped his father was either dead or had flown. The silence from the arroyo told its own story too.

White-lipped, he made his way to it, afraid of what he was to find.

"Pop!" he shouted. "Where are yuh?"

There was no answer. He called a second time and only a throat-tightening silence rewarded him.

"They got him," he despaired, a sob in his throat. "He'd answer if he could."

With a rush he came off the bank into the wash and began to work back toward the house. He saw a man's head appear. He almost banged away at him before he realized it was only Chalk.

A moment later he found Waco under the cut bank. With a stifled cry of anguish he flung himself out of the saddle and rushed to his father's side. The blood-bathed body, the wide, staring eyes told him his answer even before he clutched the stiffening hands.

"Oh, my God," he groaned. "They got you, Pop . . . I got here too late. . . ."

He had been raised in a hard school, but there was a streak of tenderness deep-seated in him. His eyes filled with tears, and he was not ashamed of them.

Chalk came clumping up, snorting wildly. What he saw staggered him. It was seconds before he could speak.

"Snuffed him out," he gasped. "Right here in sight of the house. . . . The murderin', black-hearted rats!" The rest of what he said can not be printed here, and it deserved a better fate.

"I guess this is the way he wanted to go," Little Bill murmured. "He always said he wanted to kick off with his boots on."

"Yeh, he must have liked all this excitement at the end," Chalk agreed. "His guns is empty, Bill; kept bangin' away until the last."

Little Bill shook his head sadly.

"Me and Luther had this on our minds last night," he said. "I didn't sleep much for worryin' about him. Now you tell me what happened."

Chalk's account was to the point.

"He shouldn't have done it, Bill," he finished. "I told him so last night. It was n't up to him to kick his life away for somebody else's money——"

"You're wrong, Chalk," Little Bill broke in. "He only knew one way to play the game. We mustn't take that away from him. Luther and me will get the hombres that cooked this up. I don't care how long it takes, we'll square it in full!"

He had ridden into Bowie ahead of Tascosa and the others, as he had said he would, intending only to linger for a few minutes. Martha Southard's dark eyes had been haunting him for months. No word of his had yet acquainted her with his romantic devotion, for with becoming humbleness he believed himself quite unworthy of her. And yet, whenever he was in town, he found certain crumbs of comfort in her apparent happiness at seeing him again that sent him away to dream of her for another five or six weeks. On the trail or in some lonely cow camp he became bold enough in his thoughts to foresee the time when he would speak frankly to her.

It had been in his mind to do so this trip. His run-in with Beaudry had changed his plans and he had come in this morning hoping for no more than a word or two with her.

He had circled around town to reach home. All that had been temporarily erased from his mind. It came back to him now with startling clearness.

"What about Beaudry?" he asked. "Is he back?"

"Yeh, came in last night. Waco was talkin' to him."

"So? Was anythin' said about me?"

"Only that he had seen your outfit on the river." Chalk glanced at him shrewdly. "Was there anythin' else that should have been said, Bill?"

"Plenty, Chalk. Beaudry is out to slam me into jail."

He acquainted the old man with the facts.

"Damn his yellow hide!" Chalk cursed. "He better go slow about startin' anythin' with you with yore pa lyin' dead here! You got friends in this yere town— and that's somethin' Beaudry's got none of!"

"I don't reckon that'll stop him," said Little Bill, his face grim. "It don't matter; I ain't runnin' now —and nobody is slappin' me into jail until I get the party or parties that did this."

"It'll be around town in a few minutes that you're here," Chalk warned him. "The shootin' must have been heard down the street."

"Let 'em come," Little Bill ground out. "Is Pop's mustang in the barn?"

"He is. Why——"

"You get him saddled pronto," the red-headed one cut him off. "I want you to go for Luther. They must be this side of Cain Springs by now. You tell him what's happened—that I want him in a hurry. Luther will know what to do. You get goin' right now, Chalk. I'll carry Pop up to the house."

He saw the old man glance at Six-gun, standing patiently, reins dangling over his head.

"It would save time if I took him," said Chalk.

Little Bill shook his head.

"You can't ride him, Chalk."

"I could handle him. You don't have to worry about my leg."

"It ain't that. He's my horse; nobody ridin' him but me."

"Well, I ain't hankerin' to ride him," Chalk said sharply. "I'm superstitious of them claybanks. Like as not this would never have happened but for you ownin' that——"

"Don't say it!" Little Bill snapped. "No man's turnin' me against him! You get movin'!"

Chalk clumped away, muttering to himself. Little Bill gathered his father's body up into his arms and started up the arroyo, with Six-gun following a pace or two in the rear. The gelding nickered softly.

"I'm puttin' the blame for this where it belongs—not on you, Six-gun," Little Bill thought aloud.

Chapter VII

FANNING the little mustang with his hat, Chalk Whipple dashed out of the yard and raced away in a flash of dust. Down the street, Sam Swift and some others appeared, running toward the house. Sam hailed the old man, but Chalk thundered on without waiting to answer. It was five miles to Cain Springs, and it was his intention to get there in a hurry.

"That don't look good, him dashin' off that-a-way," Sam panted. "He's goin' for the boys, sure as shootin'!"

"Beaudry must be right for once," one of his companions flung back as they ran on. "He said it was the Sontags—come in to get Waco. They must a fetched him or Chalk wouldn't be tearin' off like that."

" 'Fraid you're right," Sam muttered. "Beaudry will never overhaul 'em if it was the Sontags."

"Him and his depities was sure crowdin' their ponies as they sailed out of town," another volunteered. "Damn near run me down!"

Through the window Little Bill saw the group of men approaching. He recognized Sam quickly. He had placed his father's body on the bed. Pausing to cover it with a sheet, he stepped to the door.

"Why, Bill, I didn't know you had got in!" Sam

exclaimed, heaving asthmatically. "Is—is anythin' wrong?"

He found the question almost unnecessary, for Little Bill's grim face was an answer in itself.

"He's dead, Sam," he said. "They got him down the arroyo a ways."

"No, you don't say!" Swift shook his head sadly and made a little clucking noise with his tongue. Usually a garrulous man, he had no words with which to express himself at a moment like this.

Save for a muttered curse or gasp of surprise the others were strangely inarticulate too. They had all been in the crowd that had shouted Waco's praises in the Longhorn the previous evening. They found it hard to believe that he was gone so soon.

"If there's anythin' we can do," Sam volunteered soberly, "you know we'll be only too willin'." He glanced at the others for corroboration. They were quick to voice it.

"I sent for Luther," Little Bill told them. "We'll have a look down the arroyo as soon as he comes and see what we can find."

"I guess it's no question but what it was the Sontags," said Sam. "Your pa didn't have no enemies other than them. Beaudry and Chilton and a couple more have fanned it out of town already, saying they was goin' to cut 'em off."

Little Bill's head went up.

"Beaudry? What does he know about this?"

"Joe here can tell you more than me. He says he

was talkin' to him," Sam replied. "What was it he said, Joe?"

"Why, I reached for my pants as soon as I heard the shootin'," the man explained. "It took me a few minutes to get down to the street. I was just turnin' the corner by the Longhorn when Beaudry and Chilton fanned it out of the alley beside the sheriff's office. I asked them what the shootin' was about. Cash yelled back that the Sontags had come in for Waco and that he was goin' to cut 'em off if he could."

"So that's the way it was, eh?" Little Bill ground out threateningly. "I'll sure look into that!"

"Why, what do you mean, Bill?" Sam inquired.

"I mean it don't go with me at all! How did he come to be on the job so quick? Looks to me like he was waitin' for it to happen!"

"Well, I ain't no great booster for Beaudry," Sam remarked. "I know if I was the sheriff of this county and I heard gunfire I'd go to the scene of the shootin' to catch my outlaws instead of tryin' to cut 'em off somewhere."

"You wouldn't if you was takin' your orders from them same outlaws," Little Bill exclaimed.

"Now, Bill,—" Sam started to protest feebly.

"Don't stall, Sam! You know you've been thinkin' it! All of you have! So why not say it? You know it's true!"

"No one's proved it yet," Swift argued.

"I'll come damn close to doin' it," Little Bill assured him, "and if I ever find out that he knew they were comin' in for Pop I'll drag his dead body through the streets of this town!"

"And I'll help you do it if you ever prove that on him!" said Sam.

By now Little Bill could see a score of men hurrying toward them.

"I don't want to talk to these people," he told Swift. "If you will, Sam, keep 'em out of here. You can tell 'em what's happened."

"Why, sure, Bill. And I'll be glad to take care of all the funeral arrangements if you'll let me. We want to pay our respects to Waco in a way that will do him proud."

"Sam, I'll sure appreciate it," Little Bill said gratefully. "I'd like to have a word with you if you'll step inside."

Swift removed his hat in respect to the dead as he entered the house.

"Sam, Beaudry doesn't know I'm here," Bill said as soon as he had closed the door. "I had some trouble with him last night. I know he's goin' to get me for it if he can. I'm goin' to tell yuh what happened."

The mayor did not attempt to hide his concern at the tale Little Bill told him.

"No question but he can make it pretty hot for you, Bill," he declared soberly. "From what I know of the law, he had a right to take your horse. I appreciate how you felt about it, but that didn't warrant your openin' up on him with a rifle—in the eyes of the law I mean. All the rest of it won't enter into the case."

"What do you think he can do?"

"He can claim an assault with a deadly weapon with intent to kill. That will mean upwards of five years for you if he makes a jury believe it. I don't figure he'll do anythin' until after the funeral. He knows how folks would take it, and there's enough feelin' against him already without that. I'll speak to him if you say so, but I don't think it would do any good, bein' the ornery skunk that he is."

"I don't want you to speak to him," Little Bill said flatly. "I wouldn't give him the satisfaction of lettin' him think I was lookin' for an out. I reckon if he didn't have a reason last night for wantin' me locked up he's got one now. If he's got a lick of sense he must know I won't quit until I know who handed it to Pop."

A wild tattoo of driving hoofs brought him to the window. Six riders were sweeping up the road in a swirl of dust, their horses flecked with foam.

His first thought was that it was Beaudry and his deputies. He saw now that it was Luther, Chalk and the whole Sawbuck bunch, with the exception of Maverick.

Chalk had met up with them a short distance out of town, for they had come on ahead of the wagon, anxious to know what was happening to Little Bill. Chalk's news had brought them into town on a slashing ride.

The crowd gathered in front of the house scattered hurriedly as they swept into the yard. They were riding the horses Beaudry had left them. They brought them to a slithering stop and slid out of their saddles with an angry flourish.

Luther looked around for his brother.

"Where's Bill?" he jerked out.

"He's inside," two or three in the crowd answered.

At that moment Little Bill opened the door. Luther and the others made a rush for it.

"Where is Pop?" Luther demanded huskily. His face was haggard-looking.

"I put him in on his bed," Little Bill answered.

Luther and Tascosa went into the bedroom together. The others stood about uneasily, their faces hard.

"You know what we all think about this," said Link Appling. "We're here to help you square it, Bill."

"We ain't got nothin' else to do until it is squared," Scotty Ryan seconded.

Their loyalty touched Little Bill. He nodded his head in token of appreciation.

Tascosa and Luther stepped out of the bedroom. There was a steely glitter in Tas' eyes.

" 'T ain't for me to say what should be done," he remarked somberly, "but Oklahoma wouldn't be big enough for the Sontags to hide in if it was left to me." He wiped his tobacco-stained mouth with the back of his hand. "You and Luther talk it over, Bill. We'll go along with yuh whatever yuh decide."

"I'm goin' to have a look down the arroyo," Little Bill informed them. "We may find some sign that will tell us what we want to know. Sam is goin' to take charge of the funeral for us, Luther. You and me can be runnin' things down a little in the meantime."

"I'm agreeable to that," said Luther. His face was wooden. "Have you seen anythin' of Beaudry?"

"Not a thing." Little Bill told him why. "He's overplayed his hand this time, Luther."

"I'll say he has!" Luther got out accusingly. "He knew it was the Sontags the moment he heard a gun bark, eh? I reckon that ain't all he knows! I figure to find out the rest of it! Ridin' out of town to cut 'em off!" he spat out with supreme contempt. "That ain't foolin' me!"

"He'd have to bring me their scalps before I'd believe him," Tascosa growled. "I'll have somethin' to say to him."

"Take my advice and go slow, Tas," Sam counseled. "He's got Bill in a bad jam if he wants to prefer charges against him. I'd kinda hold in for a day or two until you see what he intends to do about that."

"Maybe you're right," Tascosa admitted grudgingly. "But things is jest nacherally workin' toward a showdown. It can't be put off long. If you're goin' to have a look at that arroyo, I'll trail along. I ain't forgot all I knew about trackin'."

"We'll go now," said Little Bill. "Chalk and Sam can take charge of things here."

Chapter VIII

THEY found Waco's hat and then quickly found where he had rolled down into the wash. In the sandy soil it was no difficult matter to follow the way he had taken over to the cut bank.

"There's where I found him," Bill told them. "You can see the empty shells lyin' around. Blood on the bank there. . . . He must have propped himself up against it."

"No question about it," said Tascosa. He sat himself down as he imagined Waco had done. "Just what I thought!" he announced. "Your pa must have stumbled or thrown himself down before he got here. I examined him and I know the slug that killed him got him through the back."

"Looks like this is where he fell," Luther declared after moving a few feet out into the draw. "A man concealed up there on the bank couldn't have missed him at that distance."

"That's the way it was," Tas muttered gravely. "Waco figgered if he reached here he had a chance. The bank overhangs so that to git him from above a man would have had to show himself, and your pa would have marked him at least."

"We'll get up there now and see what we can find," said Little Bill.

They had to drop down the wash before they could find a place their horses would climb. Empty cartridges and the broken-down grass showed them where the killer had lain. Luther compared one of the brass shells with his own. They were identical.

"That won't tell us anythin'," he said. "Regular Remington .45 calibre shell. No blood stain up here either."

"I didn't expect to find any," Bill told him. "I want to find out how that hombre got in here and which way he went in gettin' out—and if there was some others waitin' to cover him."

"You follow me," Tascosa ordered. "Shouldn't be no trick to follow signs as plentiful as this."

On foot, leading their horses, they began moving across the flat toward a little grove of old cotton-woods that marked the site of what had once been Bowie's original boot hill.

They were not over forty minutes in reaching the trees. There they found the tracks of three or four horses.

"They was sure here to cover him if he got into a jam," Luther observed. "If you'd come in this way this mornin', Bill, you'd have run smack into 'em."

"I wish to God I had," Little Bill rasped bitterly.

Tascosa said nothing, but the glance he directed at Six-gun said eloquently enough that he held the clay-bank to blame even in this.

Mounting, they followed the tracks of the horses

until they found themselves on the heavily used road that ran from Bowie to Kingfisher. In the past few minutes a three-wagon freight outfit had passed. They could see it moving into town now.

"That stops us," Little Bill fumed, " 'cause they sure turned into the road."

"And we can't tell now how far they followed it before they turned out——"

"I don't care about that," Little Bill interrupted. "All I hoped to learn was whether one of 'em went right on into town. I don't believe Beaudry ever went out lookin' for 'em until he knew where not to look."

"Well, let's jog along as far as the old 'dobe anyhow," Tascosa suggested. "Anybody headin' for the west would most likely turn off about there. We may pick up somethin'."

Little Bill was about to consent when he became aware of a horseman hurrying in their direction.

"Whoever he is he ain't losin' no time," he murmured with growing concern.

"Yeh, usin' the quirt all right," said Tas.

In a few seconds Little Bill recognized the rider.

"Why, it's Martha!" he exclaimed with a start. "There's somethin' wrong. I never saw her crowd a horse like that before."

"Only bad news travels fast, they say," Tascosa muttered to himself.

The tenseness that tightened Martha Southard's face told them even before she spoke that she came on an urgent errand.

"Please, Bill," she interrupted as the red-haired

one started to voice his surprise at seeing her there,
"let me do the talking; you haven't a minute to waste!
The sheriff has a warrant for you and he's at your
place now trying to serve it!"

Little Bill stared at her speechlessly for a moment.
The spell of her presence was enough in itself to
tighten his throat. In her excitement he found her
more beautiful than ever, and he had only to gaze into
her eyes and see the concern in them for himself to
be rendered helpless.

"But, Martha——" he protested weakly, "I can't go
now with Pop lyin' dead at home——"

"But you must go," Martha insisted. "Sam has told
me all about last night. I'd just heard about your
father and was going to your place when Sam came
hurrying out of the courthouse. He told me where to
find you—to tell you to go; that he would look after
everything . . . Beaudry hates you. If he ever gets you
into jail you'll never get out—and you've got to get
justice for your father." She turned to Tascosa. "You
make him go, Tascosa; Beaudry will not be sheriff
long; Bill will soon be able to come back."

Tas had to get rid of his cud of tobacco before he
could answer. Being in the presence of a lady, he
turned his head respectfully before spitting it out.

"Well, Martha, I reckon they ain't no two ways
about this," he said weightily after wiping his mouth.
"Bill's got to git goin'. It's one thing for the law to
have a grudge ag'in yuh and quite another to be lan-
guishin' in jail while the hombres that put yuh there
is free to continue their deviltry." He turned to Bill.

"There ain't nothin' you can do for yore pa now half so important as what Martha has just said; that's to get him justice."

"You're right," Luther agreed. "That goes for both of us. If I had a fresh horse——"

"You can have this one," Martha offered immediately. "I know it will be all right with Paint——"

"Paint?" Bill echoed with a stab of jealousy. "What's he got to do with it?"

"It's his horse," said Martha, coloring unconsciously. "He broke her for me and brought her in the last time he came to town. I told him I couldn't accept the mare, but he insisted on leaving her with our string. She hasn't been ridden much."

Bill found a grain of satisfaction in that. He had once thought of offering Six-gun to her. That couldn't be now, but he couldn't help wondering what her answer would have been.

Out of the corner of his eye he caught a glimpse of horsemen crossing the flat. It pulled him up to sharp decision.

"We'll take the mare," he got out gruffly. "Yank that saddle off in a hurry, Luther! We've got only a few seconds to make the change, for here comes Beaudry and his bunch now! They'll see us as soon as they reach the cottonwoods!"

Martha lost no time in dismounting. Little Bill had her saddle off before Luther was ready to drop his own on the mare. Tascosa had turned to watch the posse.

"So you're the cause of all this trouble," he heard

Martha say. Out of the corner of his eyes he saw her stroking Six-gun's muzzle. "You're a beauty!"

"He's most powerful bad luck, if you ask me," Tas grumbled under his breath. "Get movin'!" he called out suddenly. "They got you located and they're sure a-poundin' leather!"

"You ready, Luther?" Little Bill jerked out hoarsely as he swung up into his saddle.

"Let 'em go!" Luther answered. He gave the mare the spurs.

"Hurry, Bill!" Martha urged, her face bloodless.

"I'm goin'," he answered. "It may be some time before I see you again, but I'll be thinkin' of you. . . . If you remember it, I wish you'd say a little prayer for Pop——"

"Good-bye——" she murmured, her eyes misting.

The powerful gelding leaped away. In ten yards Little Bill had pulled Six-gun into a distance-devouring gallop.

Chapter IX

LITTLE BILL glanced back repeatedly at the posse. He had not expected Beaudry to hang on after it became apparent that they could not be overtaken.

"Still back there, eh?" Luther asked.

"Yeh, still trailin' us, but we seem to be drawin' a little away all the time."

"We'll shake 'em off as soon as we get out of this flat country and run into a little scrub timber."

"I wasn't thinkin' of that," said Bill. "I was just wonderin' what's makin' Beaudry so anxious to grab us so suddenly. Sam thought he would hold off until the funeral was over. You can see by the way he's hangin' on now that he means business. You might think we'd just hoisted a bank."

"I suppose somebody repeated to him what you said about linkin' him up with the Sontags. He evidently figgers you can do it."

They were between three and four miles out of Bowie by now. It was their intention to intercept the Sawbuck wagon and get their rifles and blankets. According to their calculations, Maverick should be nearing Cain Springs.

"We'll have to get some grub off Maverick," said

Little Bill. "We'll head west then and make ourselves pretty hard to find for a few days."

Luther nodded and conversation died again for another ten minutes. Bill had thoughts of Martha Southard to temper his bitterness; Luther was not so fortunate.

"I'll never forget her comin' to warn me," Bill murmured to himself. "Some people are sure to talk me down and give me a bad name for this. I don't care what they say if it don't turn her against me."

The country was beginning to change. The treeless level plain southwest of Bowie was giving ~   ~o rolling, scrub-covered hills. Bill turned in his saddle to find Beaudry and his posse far behind.

"We won't change our course until we get in among the scrub," he advised Luther. "They'll think we're headin' for the Strip. If they keep after us, that's the way they'll go, stayin' close to the Cimarron bottoms."

In a few minutes they lost sight of the posse and swung to the south for the springs. The gelding hadn't raised a sweat. The mare Luther was riding was flecked with lather. She had evidently been on hard grain for weeks and had had far too little exercise. She was strong, however, and would toughen up in a hurry.

An old stone house that dated back to the days of the Texas trail stood under the cottonwoods at Cain Springs. The Sawbuck wagon stood drawn up before it as Luther and Little Bill rode in. Maverick was watering his horses. He dropped his bucket on catching sight of them and stared his surprise.

"What's the idea of this?" he demanded banteringly. "You git chased out of town?"

"That's exactly what happened," Bill informed him. "A lot of things have taken place since I saw you last, Maverick. We're here to get our rifles and blankets. Want you to make us up a sack of grub too."

"Hunh?" Maverick grunted as their soberness was communicated to him. "Why, you boys mean it!"

"We do, for a fact," said Little Bill as he and Luther pulled their rolls out of the wagon. "I don't know how much time we've got; just shake up anythin' that's handy. We can talk while you're gettin' it ready. You tell Tascosa we took this sack of cartridges."

Maverick threw some stuff together as Little Bill acquainted him with what had happened. Luther had walked back to a little ridge twenty-five yards beyond the house. He could see for some distance from the crest of it.

"I'm sorry to hear all this, Bill," Maverick asserted with a great wagging of his head. "You're goin' up against a bad bunch in them Sontags. I know some of 'em. You look out for Grat. He's the kind what kills just to see a man kick. You got any plans?"

"We'll make our plans as we go along, Maverick. If you've got that sack ready I'll tie it on my saddle."

"There it is! I'll give yuh a little tobacco if——"

He didn't finish. Luther was running toward them.

"Bill, they're comin'!" Luther shouted. "They got this place surrounded! The best thing we can do is git our horses inside the house and stand 'em off! Maybe we can slip out tonight!"

"Grab your horse then and get him in!" Bill snapped out. "You get that wagon rollin' out of here, Maverick! There'll be hell to pay in a muinte!"

Neither the mare nor the gelding wanted to enter the house. It took precious seconds to get them inside. Maverick had leaped to the seat of the wagon and was lashing the team into a run.

Inside the old stone house, roofless for many years, Little Bill and Luther waited grimly for the attack. To their surprise, minutes passed without bringing a shot or summons to surrender. The creaking of the wagon had died away in the distance.

"You couldn't have been mistaken, Luther?" Bill asked.

"Not a chance! They're here! Crawlin' up behind that ridge like as not!" He flicked a glance at his brother. "You got any idea what we're goin' to do if they try to rush us?"

"They'll have a time gettin' us out of here," said Bill.

"That ain't answerin' me! Are we goin' to shoot to kill—that's what I want to know! You can figger what it means if we do. It will put us outside the law for the rest of our lives."

"I know it," Little Bill muttered gloomily. "Our hand is bein' forced, but it ain't my idea to shoot these men down if it can be helped; though killin' is what they need. They won't make much of an attempt to take us alive. If he can wash us out legally, Beaudry will do it."

"No doubt of it, Bill. With no witnesses around, I'm

thinkin' we wouldn't git very far if we walked out of here with our hands in the air. It's askin' a lot of a man to expect him to hold off when he's facin' a bunch that's dead set on wipin' him out. But that's what we've got to do."

Luther stationed himself to defend the door. Little Bill took the window. In just a second or two, Beaudry hailed them.

"We got you birds dead to rights!" he yelled. "I'm callin' on yuh to give yourselves up! I've got a warrant for yuh, Bill Stillings! Yuh better throw your guns away and walk out with your hands up! Do yuh hear me?"

"We hear yuh all right!" Bill answered. "We ain't givin' ourselves up to you, Beaudry!"

"You're resistin' arrest!" Cash yelled. "If you ain't out of there in ten seconds we'll smoke yuh out!"

He counted ten. It was the signal for a crashing volley. The slugs ricocheted wickedly off the stone walls.

"They're all behind the ridge," Bill told Luther. "Don't get too near the door; they've got their guns trained on it!"

For the next twenty minutes the posse poured a hail of lead into the house. The air began to reek with the acrid fumes of burnt powder. The blue haze of gun smoke drifted in through the open door and window. Six-gun and the mare didn't like it at all. Little Bill and Luther still held their fire.

"We better show 'em we know how to shoot," Luther argued, "or they'll think we don't intend to.

First thing we know they'll try to reach that tree out there. If they do, it'll be pretty hot for us in here."

The tree to which he referred stood halfway down the slope. A man could reach it from the top in ten strides. On the heels of another withering volley, Blackie Chilton leaped over the crest and made a rush for the cottonwood. From the house two streams of fire flashed through the haze.

Chilton changed his mind in a hurry. In his anxiety to get back to cover he whirled so swiftly that he threw his gun away. He disappeared behind the ridge in a dive that landed him on his nose.

"Didn't touch him," Luther grinned owlishly, "but I bet he felt them slugs burnin' him as they went by."

"They'll try it again," said Little Bill. "Come at us in two ways the next time. If this smoke gets much thicker we won't know what we're shootin' at."

Beaudry divided his forces now, as Bill had foreseen. Ten minutes later three of his men leaped over the crest to the left of the house and made a dash for the springs. Another ran for the tree that Chilton had failed to reach. This man was turned back too, but the other three made the rock watering-trough beside the springs.

"They crease you, Bill?" Luther demanded anxiously as he saw a trickle of blood run down his brother's cheek.

"No, just a chip of rock caught me," Little Bill muttered. He realized that the three men at the trough could advance under cover of a fusillade from their companions. "Things ain't workin' out so well for us," he went on. "If those gents out there make a rush for the door we'll have to drop 'em or it'll be all over with us."

"It ain't what we want to do," Luther murmured gravely, "but there's some things you can't walk away from. I'm afraid I winged the hombre that tried to reach the tree."

"I'm goin' to try to get 'em out from behind the trough," Bill told him. "You hold Six-gun steady there in the corner so I can stand on the saddle. I'm goin' to fire over the top of the wall. They'll be right under my gun. I'll give 'em a chance to back away if they want it. If they don't take it, I'm goin' to bust 'em, Luther."

"Get up there and Beaudry will pick you off from the ridge!" Luther warned. "Don't you try it! I been thinkin' things over, Bill. Maybe we made a mistake not to parley with them."

"What sense would there be in doin' it? He wants our hides and nothin' else!"

"I'm goin' to talk to him just the same. It'll give this smoke a chance to rise."

"You're wastin' your time," Little Bill protested impatiently. "But you go ahead if yuh want to."

Beaudry answered Luther's hail.

"Are yuh ready to come out?" he demanded.

"What sort of a proposition will you make us if we do?" Luther yelled back. "We got plenty ammunition left."

"So have we," Cash informed him, "and we got plenty of time! But I'll make a deal with yuh, Luther, if you'll come out."

"What sort of a deal?" Luther inquired sceptically.

"It ain't you we want," Beaudry returned. "I'm inclined to be reasonable. Just walk out of there———"

At that moment the three men at the trough made a rush for the door. Beaudry's willingness to talk had been just a ruse to divert the attention of the two men in the house.

Little Bill cried a warning, but before Luther could leap back a bullet tore a ragged gash across his cheek.

"Pump that gun!" Bill screamed at him. He was firing madly himself.

The three men fell back, one of them with a slug in his shoulder.

"That settles it!" Little Bill raged. "They'd shoot yuh down even when yuh was parleyin' with 'em! It's them or us now, and we're shootin' to kill! Just bang away at anythin' that shows!"

Chapter X

THE gunfire from the ridge was almost continuous now. It said plainer than words that Beaudry was getting ready to rush the house.

"We better do somethin' about this," Bill told Luther. "I'm goin' to drive those hombres back from the trough or come mighty close to it."

Although Luther protested, Little Bill made him hold Six-gun now as he stood up on the seat of his saddle.

He was seen from the ridge as soon as he poked his rifle barrel over the top of the wall. The slugs began to ping and ricochet off the wall all about him, but in some miraculous way he escaped being hit.

His own gun began to bark as he opened up on the men crouched down behind the trough. Although they flattened themselves to the ground, he could see them.

Suddenly one of them let out a yell of pain, and flinging himself to his feet, beat a precipitate retreat.

The others did not linger long.

"Well, I sure smoked them out of there," Bill muttered laconically as he slid down beside Luther.

Luther flashed an incredulous glance at him.

"Wonder those gents on the ridge didn't make a sieve out of yuh," he grumbled.

Suddenly it was still. The minutes dragged by without a shot being fired.

The better part of an hour passed.

"Mighty still," said Luther. "You don't think they've drawn off?"

"They're still there," Little Bill answered. "I'll prove it to yuh."

He stuck his hat on his rifle barrel and held it up to the window. It was riddled instantly.

"That didn't git 'em anywhere," Luther grinned. His face was a gory sight. He cocked an eye at the sun. It was getting hot in the old house. He saw that it still lacked an hour of noon. "It's goin' to get hotter in here," he said. "We'll be wantin' water before the afternoon's gone." The springs would have been just as accessible a mile away as at the door.

"The horses will need it more than us," Little Bill returned. "It'll make it tough for us tonight. Sure as fate when we try to get 'em out they'll smell water and begin to act up. It'll give our play dead away."

"We may have to go without 'em," Luther suggested.

Bill said no. "We wouldn't have a chance on foot."

It wasn't long before the posse's guns opened up again. They kept up a desultory fire for a quarter of an hour. Suddenly then they began to bang in earnest. It dwarfed what had gone before.

"Sounds like they'd got reinforcements," said Luther.

It was a moment or two before they realized that the slugs were no longer spattering against the walls.

The posse seemed to have dropped back. In the course of a few minutes the heavy firing had moved completely away from the springs.

Luther and Little Bill stared at one another in growing amazement.

"What do you make of that?" Luther jerked out.

"I don't know. It may be a trick to encourage us to make a run for it. I'm goin' to climb up on Six-gun and have a peek over the wall."

"You be right careful," Luther urged. Then a moment later: "Do yuh see anythin'?"

"Why, that's Link out there!" Little Bill cried. "He's ridin' this way! Looks like that's Scotty with him!"

Luther ran outside recklessly.

"It's them all right!" he yelled. "Hey, Link!—Scotty!"

"Yee-ah!" they screeched as they dashed up to the springs.

Little Bill ran out to greet them.

"What's the meanin' of this?" he demanded. "What are you boys doin' here?"

"What do yuh think we're doin'?" Link countered. "We didn't lose no time gettin' here when Maverick came in with word that Beaudry had you cornered."

"We just handed our respects to him," Scotty drawled. "They're fannin' it away from here now."

"Not all of 'em," Link corrected. "One is layin' up there in the sage. Git your horses out of the house, boys, and we'll look things over."

"You damn fools!" Little Bill stormed. "What did yuh want to mix in this for? All of yuh here?"

"All but Tas; we figgered he was too old to take a hand in a runnin' fight," said Link.

On the ridge they met Tonto Baker and Maverick. The two men were staring at something in the brush. Their faces were glum, for now that the excitement was over they were beginning to realize where they stood.

Little Bill pulled up alongside them to stare at the lifeless thing on the ground. It was a moment or two before he spoke.

"Anybody know who he is?" he asked.

"It's Frenchy Le Breton," said Link. "It was me who got him. If his aim had been a little better it would have been the other way around. I rode up this little knoll and he cut down on me."

"Just better leave him there," Bill advised. His mouth was hard as he turned away. Link glanced at him sharply.

"I hope you ain't sore about this, Bill," he said. "It was either him or me."

"I ain't sore about nothin', Link. How could I be? Yuh got Luther and me out of a bad jam. That ain't what's in my mind at all. I just wonder if yuh realize that it means . . . that we're all outside the law now. We ain't got only a crooked sheriff against us, but every peace officer in Oklahoma as well. In twenty-four hours there'll be a price on our heads."

They had nothing to say as Bill led the way back to the springs.

"We'll water our horses and pull out of here at once," he told them. "Best thing to do is to head for the North Fork and work out into No Man's Land; we ain't safe this side of there now."

His gloomy view of things began to get on Luther's nerves.

"See here, Bill," he burst out angrily, "ain't no use in goin' on that-a-way! We did everythin' we could to keep from spillin' blood here. I never wanted to drift into outlawry. Now Beaudry has pushed us into it. Since that's the case, I intend to git even without wastin' any time. Pop got it, and we'd have got it but for the boys here. If the law—in the face of all that—can make me an outlaw, I say let it!"

There was nothing more to be said. Circumstance had burned their bridges behind them and they could only go on. Reckless, strangers to fear, they rode away from Cain Springs strangely subdued and helpless. Needing a leader, they found him in Little Bill.

No one knew the country better than they. For two days they followed the North Fork into the almost uninhabited region to the west. If they were pursued they failed to catch a glimpse of their pursuers.

From Wednesday to Friday they went without food. They were also without money. Something had to be done. So about noon on Saturday they rode into Scott's Station. There was just a backwoods store there. They drew up in front of it and Little Bill and Tonto Baker went in to see what Scott would let them have for Bill's watch.

Ike Scott had seen his share of outlaws. He was instantly aware of the six rough-looking men, all heavily armed, their manner desperate, who drew rein at his hitch rack. He was alone in his store. It imposed no handicap on him. Without wasting any time in deciding what to do, he reached for the sawed-off shotgun he kept under the counter for just such emergencies. As Little Bill and Tonto stepped through the door he flung the gun to his shoulder and fired.

Not knowing what they faced in entering the store, Bill and Tonto came in with their eyes alert. As Scott threw his gun into position they dropped to their knees behind a cracker barrel. A split second later a load of buckshot swept the door.

They were untouched. Before Scott could fire the second barrel, Tonto's six-gun barked sharply. Scott dropped his gun and fell across the counter.

Luther and the others came running to find the two men staring at the stiffening body. They stopped in their tracks.

Little Bill got to his feet and walked over to the counter. A glance was enough to tell him that Scott was dead.

"That makes it complete," he muttered gloomily. "This is a grudge the law won't forget."

"What happened?" Luther demanded huskily. "I was watchin'; I didn't see you go for your guns or do anythin' to bring this on."

"We didn't," Tonto declared soberly. "We didn't

do nothin' nor was there a word said. He just threw that shotgun to his shoulder and began to blaze away."

"I'm afraid we did more than plenty," said Little Bill.

"Why, yuh mean I shouldn't have dropped him?" Tonto demanded incredulously. "What else could I have done? He would have got us both with that second barrel!"

"Oh, I ain't findin' fault," Bill answered. "Reckon you're right, Tonto; you couldn't have done nothin' else. We're all outside the law, and there ain't nothin' for us to do but realize that it's the other fellow or us from now on."

They helped themselves to what food they could carry. With greater deliberation than they had shown since leaving Cain Springs, they mounted and rode away.

They had little to say to each other. Little Bill was the most glum of all. He could not put the thought of Martha Southard out of his mind. He found a bittersweet satisfaction in recalling how she had rushed to his side to warn him against Beaudry. Certainly her concern for him had sprung from something warmer than friendship.

It made him realize how great was his loss in losing her. That he had lost her forever, that the events of the past few days had removed her from his world as surely as death could have done, he could no longer doubt. Whatever Martha's feeling toward him, she would not be permitted to brood over it alone for long. Paint would see to that.

"I don't know as I can blame him for that," he told himself. "I can't expect Martha to string along with me now. I'd be the last one in the world to ask it of her. I don't know what lies ahead of me, but it sure ain't goin' to be nothin' for a girl like her to share."

Chapter XI

IT WAS a comparatively easy matter to lose one's self in the almost impenetrable brakes of scrub oak and buck brush in the Strip. But water was needed as well as cover.

At the end of several days they found a place that suited them. Others had been there before. There was even a brush corral that some rustling gang had built years past.

Little Bill looked the ground over carefully and from such sign as he could discover, decided that a month or more had passed since anyone had camped at this hidden spring. Reassured that they were safe for the time being, they went into camp.

There was some game in the brush, but to fire a gun was to announce their presence not only to any prowling marshal but to other wanted men like themselves, and that might mean the Sontags, for they had no way of knowing how close they were to Smoke and his long riders. So their guns were silent. Link took Little Bill to task over it.

"I didn't know we was walkin' wide of Smoke," he said. "I figgered the sooner we met up with 'em the better we'd like it."

"We'll meet up with 'em, sure enough," Bill answered, "but I don't aim to give 'em a chance to jump us. If I can, I'm goin' to be the one to pick the time and place; not Smoke. It's somethin' that will only be done once, and it's got to be done right when we do it."

"What do yuh mean by all that?" Luther demanded.

"I mean we ain't strong enough for a showdown yet. Outside of you and me and Link none of us owns a first-class rifle. We need ammunition too."

"I'd like to know where we're goin' to git all them things," Link argued.

"We'll get 'em," Bill answered him. "I'm figgerin' things out. We need money, and there's only one way I know of that men in our position can get it."

"You mean hoistin' a bank?" Luther queried, his mouth grim.

The question was unnecessary, for they understood him well enough.

"That's what I mean," the red-haired one echoed gravely. "It ain't a case of its bein' what we want to do. As I figger it, we ain't got no choice at all, unless we want to walk in and give ourselves up. You know if we do that we'll all end up down in Fort Smith with a rope around our necks."

"That's a fact," Scotty Ryan agreed. "As far as the law goes we couldn't be any worse off than we are now."

The others, save Luther, nodded owlishly. He was staring at something off in the brush. The others caught his preoccupation.

"What is it?" Little Bill questioned sharply.

"There's a man out there," Luther replied. "He's crawled behind that big gum tree."

They reached for their guns in a hurry.

"Just keep him covered," Bill snapped out. "I'll work out to the right a ways and get the meanin' of this. If he breaks cover and won't stand, you let him have it. No foolin' about this!"

He and every man in camp were instantly suspicious that the law had caught up with them already. Barring that they were agreed that the man Luther claimed to have seen cautiously working his way through the brush was a Sontag spy, for they took it for granted that since Beaudry had failed to rub them out Smoke would waste no time in trying it.

Prepared to shoot it out to the finish, if it developed that the Sontags were present in force, they strained their eyes for a glimpse of moving object.

They saw nothing however. Little Bill began to glide away noiselessly. He had not gone thirty feet when he was hailed from behind the gum tree.

"Put away your hardware, Bill," the stranger called out. His tone was friendly. "It's Latch Shively. I was jest bein' a might careful about findin' out who you was before I walked into yore camp."

The voice sounded familiar enough, but Little Bill did not lower his rifle.

"If that's you, Latch, show your face," he ordered.

A year and more had passed since he had last laid eyes on the man who stepped out from behind the tree, but he recognized him instantly.

Latch was a little man, not much bigger than Little Bill himself; upwards of fifty now, his eyes watery and the mildness of his manner emphasized by a long, drooping mustache. It was an impression that was entirely misleading, for Latch had been living outside the law for seven years or more and was wanted for a score of bank robberies and train hold-ups.

He had ridden with one band of long riders after another, for outlaw gangs were continually disintegrating as the U. S. marshals made successful war on them. Inevitably, the remnants joined other gangs. If they escaped being rubbed out without warning, they soon found themselves hunted down all over again. Latch had had no better luck than the run of outlaws. Little Bill had last heard of him as a member of the Yeager gang that had all but been wiped out in a two-day·gun fight with a posse of marshals, a month back.

"Well, it's you, sure enough, Latch," he said. "Come on in."

He was honestly glad to see him, for here was a tried and true hand who would be useful in any emergency. As for Luther and the others, they felt quite as he did about it. Some had slight acquaintance with Shively; the others at least knew him by reputation.

"Latch, you look a bit seedy," Little Bill said banteringly as Maverick put the coffee pot on the fire.

"Yeh, I fergot to have my pants pressed this mornin', sure enough," Latch chuckled, with a rueful glance at his faded butternut jeans. "Fact is, Bill, I came out of this last fracas with nothin' but my guns and my appetite. I jest about been livin' on roots for a week." He cast an appraising eye over the camp. "You boys seem to be travelin' pretty light too. . . . You ain't all out of grub, be yuh?"

"No, we got enough for a day or two," Bill grinned mirthlessly. "We're figgerin' on movin' directly." He broke off only to add after a moment's pause, "I reckon you've heard how things stand with us."

Latch nodded.

"I daresay I've heered the most of it," he said, "and I've read the rest."

"What do yuh mean by that?" Link asked. "I didn't know you'd left any forwardin' address for your newspaper."

One or two laughed at the little pleasantry.

"Maybe he got it special delivery," Tonto Baker observed.

"Mebbe I did at that," Latch declared, wagging his head. "Leastwise it was delivered special by some depity sheriff or marshal."

From his pocket he drew out a soiled and folded piece of paper. When he had it spread out they saw that it was a poster that said in big black letters:

WANTED

FOR MURDER

$500 Reward for the Arrest or Information Leading to the Arrest of the Following

Their names and descriptions followed. The poster bore the printed signature of Cash Beaudry, sheriff of Cimarron County.

Their faces hardened as they read it to the last line. It told them no more than they had expected, but seeing it in black and white was a conclusive confirmation that affected every one of them.

"Where did you get this?" Little Bill asked.

"Oh, I tore it off a fence on the Blackhawk road," Latch told him. "They've got 'em up everywheres."

"I reckon they have," Bill muttered. His voice was cold and harsh. He stared at the poster for a moment. "Both of those men had guns in their hands and was blazing away at us when we dropped them. You can't call that murder. But hell's fire, that's only an excuse to rub us out. There's somethin' behind all this that don't appear on the surface. Beaudry has got it in for us on his own account; but that's only half of it. I reckon you heard that the Sontags got Pop."

"I heerd that somebody got him," said Latch. He shrugged his shoulders doubtfully. "Mebbe it was the Sontags got him."

"Couldn't have been no one else," Luther put in. "Beaudry is takin' his orders from Smoke. Reckon you know that, Latch."

"Mebbe I know it," the newcomer admitted. He stroked his ragged mustache thoughtfully. "I could tell yuh things; but I won't."

"It ain't necessary," Little Bill said bluntly. "The Sontags know us, and they know this country ain't big enough to hold them and us any more. That's why

Beaudry tried to wipe us out at Cain Springs. I'm tellin' yuh we aim to remember a few of them things."

Maverick called them to eat. The pickings were slim.

"Better dish up some more," Bill told him. "It's only puttin' things off to no purpose to try to piece things out to last an extra meal or two. The quicker we git to the bottom of the pot the sooner we'll be movin'."

There was a murmur of approval from the others.

"The motion seems to have been carried," said Maverick. He began to slice up the last of their bacon.

They had little to say as they ate. The meal finished, Little Bill built himself a cigarette. His manner was thoughtful.

"Latch," he said without preamble of any sort, "how'd you like to ride with us?"

The outlaw did not seem surprised at the question.

"I aimed to git around to that myself," he answered. "Fact is, it would suit me first-rate, Bill."

"You say that knowin' how things stand between us and the Sontags; that there's a showdown comin' that 'll be a showdown?"

"That don't bother me," the little man answered without hesitation. "I never got no favors from the Sontags, nor asked fer any. I can't say they ever crowded me any, either. But I'll say this, if I throw in with yuh I'll go all the way."

"We'd like to have yuh," Bill told him.

"There's jest one thing holdin' me back," said Latch. Every eye around the fire was focused on him sharply as he hesitated momentarily. "And it's jest this, boys; I ain't alone. Two of us came out of the big fight at Black Hawk. I got the Cherokee Kid with me and I don't feel I can walk out on him."

There was instantaneous tightening of their mouths at mention of the Cherokee Kid's name.

"We don't want none of him," Link Appling declared hostilely. "Every bunch he's ridden with has been wiped out, and I've heard it said it wa'n't no accident that he never was present when the blow-off came."

"I've heard it too," said Luther. "I didn't know he was ridin' with you and the Yeagers, but if he's come through again without even bein' creased I'd say it would take a deal of explainin'."

Scotty and Tonto also had a word to say against the man.

"I think you're wrong, boys," Latch said when they had finished. "I've heerd some of this talk against him, but I don't put no stock in it. Cherokee has been with us for four months, and I know he's all right. You needn't worry about him not bein' creased. Three or four days back I thought I'd have to ampytate his leg. I finally dug the slug out. He's comin' around okay and if he gits a little grub under his belt he'll be all right directly."

"Where have yuh got him?" Little Bill asked. He had yet to express an opinion about Cherokee.

"Beyond this rise about a mile," said Latch.

"You afoot?"

"No, we got horses, such as they are. It'll be a day

or two before the Kid can do much ridin'. I don't want to sway you one way or t'other about him, Bill, but he ain't a bad man to take along. He's a little too quick on the trigger when he's likkered up. You can handle him though."

Little Bill took his time about answering and when he spoke at last it was to voice a question, and it was sufficiently startling to make them set up stiffly.

"Latch—ain't it a fact that Cherokee and Cash Beaudry used to pal together when they was both workin' for the old Cross T outfit?"

It was something that the others had forgotten or never knew.

"I didn't know 'em in them days," Latch said frankly, "but I take it yo're right, and that's jest what makes me think Cherokee ought to be the man fer you. Since your memory is so good, mebbe you'll recall that soon after Cash managed to git hisself elected sheriff that Cherokee showed up in Bowie and struck him for a job. He didn't git it fer some reason——"

"Most likely because Smoke said no," Luther observed. "There's nothin' wrong with Smoke's hearin'."

"Mebbe that was the reason," the little fellow agreed. "Whatever it was it's turned Cherokee ag'in 'em—and that ought to be enough fer you."

"It is!" Little Bill exclaimed in a sudden decision. "You fetch him in, Latch. If he wants to take orders from me, he's ridin' with us."

Luther heaved himself to his feet.

"Why, Bill, you can't mean that!" he exclaimed sullenly. "Link had it right; we don't want none of

Cherokee. Give him all the best of it and he's still a Jonah."

A glance told Little Bill that he stood alone in this difference of opinion. He met it calmly.

"I don't put no stock in Jonahs," he declared without raising his voice. "That's just a piece with Tas's talk about the claybank bein' bad luck. The sooner you git that sort of nonsense out of your heads the better off you'll be. If there's anybody here that don't like my way of doin' things he's free to go; but if I'm givin' orders, I'm a givin' 'em. You bring Cherokee in, Latch."

After Shively left they continued to sit around the burned-out fire. They had shifted their position, however, until Little Bill sat alone. He was aware of it and what it meant. Conversation had died long since. It did not appear to disturb him.

"So you've got it all figgered out that I'm makin' a mistake, eh?" he queried without warning. "Appears to me it's about time you boys began to use your heads."

He spoke without a trace of rancor.

"Some of us reckon that's what you ought to be doin'," Luther answered.

"That's what I am doin'!" The red-haired one's manner was suddenly hard as steel. "Latch will come in mighty handy. There can't be no fault found with him. As for Cherokee—he ain't foolin' me for a second. He'll double-cross us the first chance he gits."

"What!" several gasped in unison. They couldn't understand him even yet.

"You mind explainin' yourself?" Luther asked with a flash of temper.

"If it needs explainin'—no!" Little Bill shot back at him. "A man ain't one thing today and somethin' else tomorrow, and they don't pal together unless they're cut from the same pattern. I know Cherokee and Beaudry used to be mighty thick. I wouldn't have to know anythin' worse against him to put me on my guard. If you think I'd trust one any farther than I would the other, you're plumb crazy!"

It left them staring at him in tongue-tied surprise for a moment. Finally Link spoke.

"Then why be yuh invitin' him in?" he asked.

"He's got information we need, that's why. If he's really gunnin' for Beaudry and the Sontags he can tell us a lot. It'll be up to us to decide whether he's lyin' or not . . . Just be smart enough not to let him know what we're thinkin'. Keep your eyes on him right along. The first crooked move he makes will be his last."

Chapter XII

THEY had to give Cherokee a hand to get him down from his horse. He thanked them with a grin that showed his even, white teeth. If Latch had apprised him that there was some feeling against him in the camp, he gave no sign of it.

"That laig is still pretty sore," he said apologetically.

He was tall and thin enough to be tubercular. His hair and eyes were as black as a raven's wing. He claimed to be a quarter blood, but his features were all Indian.

"Shuffle up some food for this man, Maverick," Little Bill suggested.

Cherokee thanked him with another grin and proceeded to roll a cigarette. He did it deftly. There was a catlike suppleness about him that was noticeable even in the movement of his fingers.

"I've told him a few things," Latch volunteered. He jerked his head in the Kid's direction. "He likes the idee."

"Yeh, I do," Cherokee drawled without bothering to look up, "specially if you're settin' yourselves for a showdown with certain parties. It runs right along with what I've had on my mind for a few months. I've been savin' a place on my gun for a notch or two. I've got the gents all picked out, I don't mind tellin' yuh."

"I take it you're referrin' to Beaudry and Smoke," Little Bill observed.

"Beaudry and Smoke and the whole damn Sontag bunch!" Cherokee whipped out with sudden viciousness. "I don't forget my grudges, not when they're handed me by men who I thought was my friends!"

"You was never over particular about choosin' yore friends," Maverick muttered as he hovered over the fire. The bluntness and unfriendliness of the remark were without effect on Cherokee.

"You're dead right there," he drawled. "I used to think if a man was on the level with his pals that it didn't matter what else he was. But I'm learnin'. Somethin' will be done about it, too, whether I tag along with you boys or go it alone."

"That's for you to decide," said Little Bill. "I'd like to know your answer."

"I'd give it to you in a second if I thought I could hold up my end. But you see the shape I'm in. I'm afraid I wouldn't be much good to you."

Cherokee could not have said anything better calculated to improve their opinion of him. An immediate evidence of better feeling was reflected in Maverick's tone as he told the Kid to come and get it.

"It ain't much," he said, "but you'll find it fillin'."

Cherokee did not have to be asked a second time.

"See him put it away!" Latch chuckled. "I tell yuh he's as tough as bull hide. Three, four days from now he'll be as sassy as ever."

"But that'll be three or four days," Cherokee said between mouthfuls. "I understood you to say that these boys was movin' right away. If that's the case they may be throwin' lead by this time tomorrow. I take it they know where to look for the Sontags."

It called for an answer and Luther and the others waited for Little Bill to voice it.

"It is a fact we are pullin' away from here this afternoon," said he, "but we're just goin' to take it easy and drift up to the Kansas line. The Sontags don't figger in our plans until we finish a little business we got ahead of us."

Cherokee's answer was a wide grin. Whether he was pleased or relieved it was impossible to tell, for his grin was a tell-nothing parting of the lips that left his swart face an inscrutable mask.

"That sounds suspiciously like business with a bank," he remarked flippantly.

"I reckon it'll git to that," Little Bill snapped out, his tone sharp enough to be a rebuke. "I aim to go over the line by myself. The rest will hide out some-where. I may be gone a day or two. When I git back we'll know what we're goin' to do."

"If Jake Creek is in the general direction you're headin' for," Latch spoke up, "we won't have no trouble about keepin' under cover and gittin' some grub. We can go to Reb Leflett's ranch. I've done business with him. He'll take us in and we can make a deal for a hoss or two."

"That'll work out all right," Bill said thoughtfully. He spoke as though his plans were more definite than he cared to say. "I know just about where Leflett's place is located. If we leave here in the next hour we ought to be on Jake Creek soon after sun up."

"Easy enough!" Latch assured him.

Little Bill turned to the Kid.

"What have yuh got to say to that, Cherokee? Is it too much ridin' for yuh?"

"I can make it as far as the creek, all right," the latter replied readily. "I know Latch is dead set on throwin' in with you boys. Suppose I trail along with you as far as Leflett's place. If my laig ain't right by the time you're ready to pull out from there, why, just leave me behind. That ought to work out about right for all of us."

Again he had said the right thing. No one could find fault with what he proposed.

They smoked another cigarette or two and then began to break camp. Traveling as light as they were it was the work of only a few minutes.

In single file they headed north. Save for Latch and Cherokee they were a sober-faced lot. It was a journey such as none of the others had ever set out on. The crashing climax it was to reach, with their lives hostage to its success or failure, was still miles and days away, but as they left the springs behind their thoughts ran ahead of them. The possibilities of that brief half an hour or less that must elapse between the time they rode into some town and dashed out, clutched at them. Their minds held in a vise, they lived over every second of it.

It left them tight-lipped, short of speech and sharp

tempered. If they came to a rise or a stretch of open country, one rode ahead and the rest held back until they knew the way was clear. They saw no one, but their trained eyes warned them that they often crossed trails that were less than a day old.

Toward sunset they reached a tiny creek. Even Latch knew of no name for it. They watered their horses and drank their fill. Maverick had nothing better to offer them than a meager helping of beans and a cold flapjack apiece. They did not risk a fire.

It had been necessary to help Cherokee out of his saddle again. He had not complained during the long ride.

"How are you makin' it?" Little Bill asked, as he sat down beside him.

"Oh, I'll make it all right," the Kid answered. "You don't have to hold back on my account."

For all his words, his face had a drawn look that said plainly enough that he was racked with pain.

Little Bill had been watching him furtively for the last two or three miles, for he had sensed an undue alertness in Cherokee. Now that they were out of the saddle and had had a bite to eat, the others had stretched out comfortably on the ground. But not the Kid. He sat up stiffly and his black eyes were seldom still. It called for an explanation.

Bill began to ask himself questions. His eyes narrowed unconsciously as an answer flashed in his brain.

"It can't be nothin' else," he told himself. "I'll have to run a bluff to prove it, but I'm goin' to risk it."

He turned to Cherokee.

"Be cooler this evenin'," he said; "that'll brace yuh up a little. It might ease yuh some if yuh got your boot off while we're restin' here. Just stretch your leg out a little and I'll get it off."

His tone was solicitous, but he was not concerned about the Kid's leg. As he would have grabbed the boot, Cherokee drew his leg away.

"No!" he jerked out sharply. "This ain't no place to be takin' off your boots! If you know where you are you know that's a fact."

Little Bill dissembled his satisfaction.

"Well, I don't know the name of this creek, but I know where I am, all right," he laughed. He was stretching the truth considerably. He proceeded to an even wilder surmise. "We ought to be a few miles east of the Black Grocery."

"You're within less than three miles of it!" Cherokee came back. "That's too damn close for a man with only one laig under him!"

The others were listening intently now, their attention riveted on the Kid. Most of them had heard vague, unsubstantiated rumors to the effect that, when in the Strip, the Sontags never strayed far from Black Grocery—a two-story frame building, with a barn across the way, set down out in the open on what had once been a cut-off for the old La Junta trail, winding up from New Mexico. Until Cherokee had spoken, not one of them, save Latch Shively, had any reason to believe that they were within forty miles of the place.

Only the creaking of saddle leather and the swishing of the horses' tails as they fought the flies broke the silence that had fallen like a blanket on Link, Luther and the others.

"Well, I ain't gettin' excited about that," Little Bill declared, still angling for information. He even essayed a yawn to express his utter boredom. "The Sontags may have the run of things around the Grocery. I reckon their women are there—Grat's girl and one or two others. Outside of them and a few hill-billies and nesters who manage to pick a livin' off Smoke's bunch you won't find no one there. You ought to be smart enough to know that. You been knockin' around long enough."

"Yeh?" Cherokee queried, angry in an instant. Being a blood, ridicule was something he could not stand. Finding an affront to his dignity in Little Bill's words, he was quick to take exception to it—just as the former expected. "Maybe you know more about this than me," the Kid was driven to sneer.

"I know that Smoke's too cagy to hang out there after all the talk there's been about the place," Bill answered sharply, his tone as contemptuous as Cherokee's. He was deliberately trying to exasperate the Kid now, in his quest for information. "Smoke wouldn't take no chance of bein' jumped that-a-way. I tell you if yuh had a lick of sense you'd know it!"

"Jump him, eh?" Cherokee burst out fiercely. "Since you're so sure it can be done why don't you try it yourself? You won't get beyond that low ridge off there to the west before you'll be stopped—and you'll be stopped cold!" His eyes had narrowed to slits. "If anybody's bein' thick around here it's you! I thought you knew what you was doin', but I'm damned if I ain't changin' my mind!"

To the listening men the drift of this conversation had become increasingly ominous. Their faces stony, they waited, making no move to interfere. This was Little Bill's quarrel, and they felt he could handle it, but not understanding his purpose, fully half of them held him to be in the wrong, for there was a ring of truth to what Cherokee had said that could not be denied. But the Kid was questioning Bill's leadership now, and they fully expected the red-haired one to take up the challenge. Instead, he said apologetically:

"Well, if a man can prove I'm wrong I'm always willin' to draw in my horns."

"I can prove it!" Cherokee said raspingly. "We've been spotted already—or what do you make of that column of smoke off there to the southwest? If it ain't a signal fire I'm crazy! I'll bet you my saddle it'll be answered directly!"

Little Bill whirled to study the spiral of smoke rising from the ridge, and the sudden concern stamped on his face was not feigned. Whatever satisfaction he felt over what he had got out of the Kid was more than offset for the time being by his anxiety as he saw the signal answered from a point directly west of them.

"You were right and I was wrong!" he exclaimed.

"I'll say I was!" Cherokee ground out. "Throw me on that piece of crow bait I'm ridin' and we'll fan it out of here! It ain't goin' to be healthy along this creek in half an hour!"

He extended a hand in Latch's direction, but the latter ignored it.

"Say, you never told me you had a slant like this on the Sontags," Latch muttered accusingly. His watery old eyes were as cold as ice.

"It's never been safe to say too much about 'em!" Cherokee answered defiantly. "But I'm tellin' yuh now!"

"Come on," Bill broke in, "this argument's gone far enough! We're ridin'!"

The ridge swung around to the north ahead of them. To avoid it, they took to the low hills to the east. Cherokee did not hold them back. He could ride with the best of them, and suffering though he was, he gave proof of it now.

The sun had dropped below the horizon before they pulled up to look back. Below them, far to the rear, they saw a band of horsemen.

"They pulled up too," Little Bill observed. "Reckon they know they can't overhaul us. Like as not they think we're a posse of marshals."

"Don't kid yourself," Cherokee jeered. "They've had a pair of glasses on us; they know who's ridin' in this bunch. We're stickin' together now whether we like it or not."

Chapter XIII

IT WAS just breaking day when they got their first glimpse of the willows that lined Jake Creek. On Latch's advice they kept well above the stream until they reached a high pasture, well hidden in the hills on the western bank.

"This is it," said Latch. "The house is down below among the cottonwoods."

The place was not much in the way of a ranch; Leflett had found an easier way of making a living than raising beef. A cautious, close-lipped man, who never let his right hand know what the left was doing, he was continually being commissioned by the minor gangs and lone wolves who infested the Strip to transact business for them that they were in no position to do themselves. Corn almost raised itself in the black soil in the creek bottom. Under the bluffs he had a still. For customers—they came to the door. Nothing could have been easier. So, one way or another, he did well enough for himself, though he often had to wait for his pay and seldom hesitated to advance money of his own to the strange brood that gathered under his roof. They could properly be considered bad risks, but they paid Leflett.

Little Bill and Latch told him what they wanted. A deal was made with a minimum of conversation.

"You can lay out up on the bluffs," he told them. "I got a shack up there that will hold you. I'll fix you up with some grub and see what I can do about a couple good broncs."

"We ain't got no money," Bill reminded him.

"That'll be all right," Leflett answered. "I don't know you boys, but if Latch says it's okay, that's enough. I'll take a look at this boy's leg while you're gone. See if I can't have him fixed up by the time you git back."

That evening Little Bill crossed the creek and rode into Kansas. By midnight he was far enough east to be in country through which the old Sawbuck outfit had often trailed beef south into Oklahoma. After locating a landmark or two he was able to determine exactly where he was.

"We can turn north here, Six-gun," he said to the gelding. "We've still got a long ride ahead of us."

He set a course that he held for the rest of the night. When he came to a crossroads store or small settlement he did not attempt to circle around it. To avoid suspicion he had left his rifle with Luther. He wore his .45's openly; but there was nothing in that to excite comment in a country where nine men out of ten went armed.

As a matter of routine, Kansas peace officers had surely been informed that he was wanted. But without a photographic likeness of himself to aid them in identifying him, he felt he had little cause to fear being picked up. There was always the possibility, however, that he might encounter some one who knew him.

"Time enough to worry about that when it happens," he told himself.

It was strange how these little Kansas towns that had once meant so little to him now loomed so importantly in his life. The location of a bank or hotel; the manner in which a place was set down beside a creek or out in the open; the direction in which the railroads, with their ever-accompanying tell-tale telegraph wires, ran—a hundred such things—were matters to be weighed and considered now with the greatest care.

They had once seemed trivial enough. But that had been a long time ago. Fortunately, these old Kansas cow towns, that already were saying farewell to the beef era and welcoming a new one of corn and sulky ploughs, were all more or less alike, with a main street, plank sidewalks and the usual assortment of sun-blistered, one-story frame buildings.

In the course of two days he drifted through three or four of them, looking them over, gauging the possibilities, only to decide that for his purpose they were too dangerous or offered too little.

He was moving farther north all the time. In itself, that must weigh heavily against any plans he made, for every mile that was added to their get-away lessened their chance of success.

In Reed City, however, he found a situation that was all to his liking. With care that would have done credit to Smoke Sontag or the great Red Doolin himself, he sized up the bank and the town, and went into every detail that could have any bearing on their enterprise. Thirty-six hours later he found himself safely back on Jake Creek. He had taken his time, being anxious to save Six-gun for the real riding that lay just ahead.

By the position of the sun, he knew it was the middle of the morning. He realized that he had struck the creek a mile or more below Leflett's place. Crossing the stream, he began picking his way toward the house. He had not gone far when he drew up sharply; he couldn't be sure, but he thought the breeze had carried to him the sounds of distant gunfire.

Listening intently for the sound to come again, he stood up in his stirrups. It was unmistakable this time. His jaws clicked together sharply.

"That's a fight, and a good one!" he ground out.

He headed for higher ground at once, taking it for granted that Luther and the others were in trouble.

"If Leflett's sold them out, I'll drop him for it!" he promised himself as he urged the gelding along.

It was only a few minutes before he got a distant view of the bluff on which he had left his men. The little puffs of white smoke that rose spasmodically from it told him it was indeed his outfit that was shooting it out with some one.

In another fifty yards he was able to locate the bunch that was attacking them. They were well up the bluff.

"The boys better not let 'em git any higher," he

thought. "Luther knows he can't fall back. Nothin' but a long drop to the creek behind him."

He was in sight of the house now. He had to pass it to reach the bluff. Armed with only a pair of six-guns he could not be of much assistance. It occurred to him that he might find a rifle there.

He approached it warily. At first, he thought it was deserted, but as he reached the pole corral between it and the creek, he heard a rifle crack from one of the upper windows. Making his way around the house, he saw that it was Reb Leflett himself who was doing the shooting, and he was firing at the men halfway up the bluff.

"Say, what's the meanin' of this?" Little Bill yelled at him.

"Put that hoss in the shed and git up here!" Leflett barked. "It's Grat Sontag and some hombres from the Grocery! You'll find a rifle back of the door!"

He emptied his gun as Bill ran up the stairs. There was a bag of cartridges on the floor beside Reb. He moved over slightly.

"Start throwin' it into 'em!" he snarled, his grizzled face as black as a thunder cloud in his wrath. "I'll show this pack o' weasels they can't ride in here and run things! This is neutral ground! Grat Sontag nor Smoke himself can bring his troubles to my door!"

"How'd this start?" Bill demanded.

"They rode up 'bout an hour ago. I don't know how they knew your bunch was here. Grat said he wanted 'em. I told him to forgit it and go about his business.

I thought they'd left until I heard the guns begin to bang. Yuh got 'em located?"

Bill let his rifle answer for him. He and Leflett did not have much to shoot at in the way of a target, but their fire apparently began to have some effect, for Grat and his crowd fell back a bit and for the next twenty minutes wasted ammunition recklessly without improving their position.

"How many of them is there?" Bill questioned.

" 'Bout seven or eight. Look! They're droppin' down towards us now! Got enough of this, I guess!"

It was only a few minutes before seven horsemen dashed down the slope in the direction of the house. They had their rifles to their shoulders and fired as they rode.

"Sure as you're born they're comin' after us now!" Little Bill jerked out. "We'll have our hands full holdin' 'em off!"

"Mebbe," Leflett growled. "We're damn poor shots if we don't pick off one or two of 'em before they git in. Let 'em come on a few yards more."

Whatever Grat's intentions were he changed his mind in a hurry. Luther and the others had broken cover and were racing down the bluff.

"Pump your gun!" Bill yelled at Leflett. "We'll end this right here!"

He was right. In a few seconds the Sontag crowd was in full flight. Luther and Link dashed up to the house. The others were only a few yards behind them. All were surprised to have Bill hail them from the window. His face was dripping perspiration.

"Well, you all look okay," he called out. "How'd yuh come through it?"

"Not a scratch," Cherokee answered. "They wasn't so lucky."

"That's right," Tonto seconded. "There's one of 'em up there on the bluff."

"Serves 'em right!" Leflett cried. "The dirty scuts! Grat knows he can't track a man to my place and go for his hardware. You boys step inside; the drinks is on me!"

Later, with Leflett still sputtering vitriolically over the violation of his rights, they started up the bluff.

"This may mean trouble for you," Latch warned him. "Grat ain't the kind to forget."

"I've taken care of a lot of trouble in my time," Leflett answered grimly. "I'll take care of this."

Little Bill rode up alongside Cherokee.

"You're lookin' better," he said.

The Kid nodded. "Yeh, I'm feelin' pretty good. Leflett fixed me up, sure enough."

Latch recognized the dead rider as Dib Fletcher.

"Jest a errand boy for the Sontags," he declared. "He don't mean a thing. But it's first blood for us."

Leflett stared at the dead man for a minute.

"I'll dig a ditch and roll him into it after you boys git away." He turned to Bill. "When you figgerin' on pullin' out?"

"Right away. We'll put a few miles behind us and lay up until it's dark."

"Then you got somethin' all set?" Cherokee inquired. Somehow the question didn't sound as casual as it should have.

"Yeh. It looks all right."

"You mind sayin' what it is?" the Kid persisted.

"We'll have a powwow after we pull away from here," Little Bill answered him flatly.

In less than an hour they were on their way. Latch dropped back to ride beside Bill. He had overheard the Kid's question up on the bluffs.

"Bill, you was pretty short with Cherokee. It was him that spotted Grat's bunch. He put up a whale of a fight. By rights you ain't got no cause to be suspicious of him."

"I ain't sayin' I am suspicious of him or Leflett or anyone else; but with a job ahead of us I wasn't sayin' anythin' about it until I knew we was alone and we're not losing sight of each other for a minute until it's over. There can't be no leaks that-a-way—accidental or otherwise. When we pull up this afternoon I'll make my say to the bunch of yuh and let yuh ask all the questions you mind. Cherokee ain't no right to ask for better than that."

"Reckon not," Latch mumbled. "It's jest that he's touchy about things."

"If he is he can git over it," Bill advised as they began to close up the gap between themselves and the men ahead. "Maybe it'll change his luck. Things have had a habit of goin' wrong for him; they ain't goin' wrong with this bunch if I can help it."

Chapter XIV

IT WAS long after the hills had given way to rolling Kansas prairie that Little Bill told them they could begin looking for a place in which to wait out the afternoon.

They finally pulled up on a little grassy flat, well screened by protecting cottonwoods, in a creek bend. They picketed their horses with great care. Link climbed one of the trees and studied the country about them. He saw nothing to arouse suspicion.

Luther and Maverick spread a pair of blankets on the ground.

"Make yourselves comfortable," Luther invited. "We'll be here some time."

They had yanked their saddles off their mounts. Ordinarily they would have stretched out and pillowed their heads on them. Instead, they sat up stiffly or squatted on their heels, waiting for Bill to have his say.

"Get on with it, Bill," Tonto prompted nervously.

"Just waitin' for Link to join us," Bill informed him. He was carrying his rifle cradled on his left arm. Without setting it aside he picked up a stick and cleared away the leaves on the ground in front of him and began to make marks in the black soil.

Link edged in between Scotty and Tonto before he had finished.

"I'll tell you all of it now," he said. "Just don't interrupt me till I'm done. If there's anythin' about this you don't like or understand you can say so then." First he told them that they were heading for Reed City.

He saw at a glance that neither Cherokee nor Latch liked the idea. Even Link and Luther shook their heads. The others were noncommittal, their faces wooden. They had been through Reed City and remembered vaguely that a bank stood at one of the town's four corners.

Methodically, his voice emotionless, Bill outlined his plans. Using the map he had drawn on the ground, he told them how they were to ride into town, the stand they were to take and the course they would pursue in their get-away. The location of the railroad, the town marshal's office, the fact that there would be activity at the railroad corrals—he appeared to have missed nothing.

"This Reed City bank ain't been stood up in years," he ran on. "That'll be in our favor. With half a break we'll be makin' our get-away before the town knows what's happened." He looked them over slowly. "I guess that's it," he said. "You can fire away now. . . . I see some of yuh don't like it."

"Not for a minute!" Latch exclaimed positively. "You put up the best argyment ag'in it yerself when you say that bank ain't been touched off in years. There's a reason fer it, and I can tell yuh what it is:

yuh got two railroads to cross before you can git back
to the Strip. Yuh can't beat the telegraph no matter
how fast yuh ride. By the time yuh hit the Sante Fé
yuh'll find more trouble waitin' fer yuh than yuh can
handle."

"Latch is right," Luther agreed. "I wa'n't thinkin'
so much about the railroads, but no matter how late
we ride into Reed City, if it's only ten minutes before
the bank closes, we'll have close to five hours to go
before it gits dark, and all of it out in the open. As I
remember it, there's hardly a bit of cover north of
here! . . . I tell yuh it's too far north."

"It's pretty far, all right," Link chimed in.

"Yeh?" the red-haired one got out slowly. "What
you got to say about it, Cherokee?"

"Just what's been said, together with the fact that
I can't see takin' a chance like that for what we stand
to get in Reed City. There's never no money in that
bank. We'd be lucky to walk out with two or three
thousand. That don't go far, split eight ways."

There was further talk, but it developed no addi-
tional criticism of the plan. Finally, they talked themselves out.

"All that you boys have said is true enough," Bill
admitted when they had done. He was singularly un-
perturbed. "If I didn't think we could be a little
smarter than you figger, I'd call this thing off."

"You can't outsmart the facts!" Latch declared
pessimistically.

"Maybe there's some facts you ain't considered,"
Bill returned. "It's never been my intention to come

back this-a-way. When we ride out of town we'll let 'em think we're takin' the shortest cut to the Strip, but in a mile or two we'll swing off to the east and get across these railroads before any Kansas sheriff can organize himself. In an hour's good hard ridin' we'll strike the big bend of the Cimarron. That ought to be cover enough for anybody. We'll follow the river south until we git near the line. We'll take another turn to the east then and slip down into Oklahoma between Kingfisher and Bowie. They won't be lookin' for us there. When we git as far down as the Skull we'll turn up the creek and work back into the Strip from the south. . . . That's a lot of ridin', but we got good horses, and it's about as safe as yuh can ask."

It won Luther and Link over.

"Now as for the money," Bill continued, "we'll do better than Cherokee thinks. Don't forgit they been shippin' beef for a week. . . . But shucks, whatever we git will be a stake. That's all we had in mind."

"That's right," Scotty echoed. It was the first word out of him. His old air of detachment had returned and he appeared as cool and deliberate as ever. "Accordin' to last reports this was an outfit without a dollar to its name, so we'll take what we can get and like it. It's just a waste of time to sit here and talk about it. The only question before the house is: can we make a get-away."

"That's the big question," Latch grumbled thoughtfully. "I'm almost persuaded we can. There's jest one thing I'd like to know, Bill: how are we goin' to make any time after we turn east if we don't keep to the roads? There's a lot of farms around New Stockholm. The country's pretty well fenced off."

"I know it," Bill admitted. "But they ain't got no telegraph to give us away. We'll ride right through New Stockholm. If anybody gits in our way we'll pull up for a second and tell 'em we've come to warn 'em that outlaws have robbed the Reed City bank—that they're headin' that-a-way. Before they have time to think it over twice we'll be out of town."

"Good enough!" Latch chuckled. "It'll fool them squareheads!" He shifted around to fix his attention on Cherokee. "Kid, I told you this boy had a head on his shoulders and knew how to use it. He may be new at this game, but he ain't green. Let him git his hand in and he'll be mighty hard to stop."

"I hope you're right," Cherokee said grudgingly. "If you're all set on this thing we'll go through with it. A man likes to do a little thinkin' for himself though."

"Wal, you bin doin' your own thinkin' fer a long time," Latch observed, "an it's kept you busted fer months. We'll jest let Bill do the thinkin' from now on."

There was a challenge in his words, but the Kid, realizing that he stood alone, refused to take it up.

Stretching out, some of them dozed off to sleep.

"We all ought to get a nap," Luther stated.

"Of course," Bill agreed. "You take it now. I'll wake you in an hour or two and you can spell me for a bit."

Propping himself up against a tree, he watched as

the others slept. Nothing happened to break the peacefulness of the warm, lazy afternoon. Inevitably his thoughts strayed to matters far removed from the grim business just ahead. And yet it seemed there was a connection, for they always brought him back to the grassy flat among the cottonwoods. He found it easy to understand, in so far as his thought concerned his father, Tascosa or Martha. He knew that if it were possible to change places with his father that Waco would do as he was doing. It would be Tascosa's way, too. He never questioned for a moment but what he would always have a staunch supporter in old Tas.

"I reckon Martha will stick up for me long after she ought to," he brooded. Memory of her suddenly became so sharp that he winced. He could fancy Tascosa trying to explain things to her, to win pardon for him. "I don't want it that-a-way!" he scourged himself. "That's a closed account, and every step I take just puts another nail in it!"

Fate had played many tricks on him. In the days to come things might so happen that he could see her again.

"It mustn't be," he decided. "I couldn't stand it. I'm sure to see Tas sometime, and he'll have plenty to say. Or I may run into Paint. That'll be hard enough to take."

The shadows were getting long before he awakened Maverick.

"If yuh brought anythin' along with yuh for a snack you'd better set it out for the boys," he told him. "We can be movin' soon."

Luther sat up, awakened by the low drone of their voices.

"You're takin' a few winks first, ain't yuh, Bill?" he asked.

"No, I ain't sleepy a bit. You can shake up the rest now and roll your blankets."

Silent, alert, they moved north through the star-studded night. Morning dawned, and they still rode on, always saving their horses. If they saw a distant ranch-house, they avoided it. When they had to cross a road they scrutinized it for minutes before moving on. An hour short of noon found them in an abandoned barn, two miles west of Reed City.

There was nothing to do but wait now. Cherokee got out a deck of greasy cards and played solitaire. It was a gesture; his attention was not on his game. Some of them smoked. Others walked back and forth. If they spoke it was about anything but the business in hand, and their voices were strained and off-key.

"Nerves beginnin' to snarl some," Little Bill said to himself.

The road they were to take into town was visible from the barn. Along its dusty length nothing moved. Overhead a pair of hawks sailed black against the sun. Noontime passed. Then it was one o'clock. The Kid had put away his cards. Cigarettes had been pinched out. Finally Little Bill drew out his watch and studied it thoughtfully.

"Ten minutes past two," he announced. "We can be movin'."

They welcomed the news as though it were escape in itself.

"Look to your guns; be sure they're free in the holsters," Bill advised. "Speakin' of guns," he continued after a momentary pause, and he was addressing himself to Cherokee now, even though he did not say so, "just remember this: no one gits very excited if somebody's bank is robbed. It's somethin' else when a band of men ride into a town and begin shootin' down innocent citizens. We'll git along without that. Course if we git in a jam we'll have to shoot and shoot to kill every time. But I ain't lookin' for that. After we git back to the horses we'll bang away a little just to let the town know we can throw lead if we have to. That'll pile 'em up long enough for us to git out on the prairie."

"That's sense," Latch said approvingly. "Jest how are we ridin' in, Bill. You got it all figgered out?"

"Yeh . . . At the edge of town I'll go ahead with Link, Tonto and Scotty. The rest of you tail along a couple hundred yards behind. If all goes well, we'll stall around at the hitch-rack at the side of the bank until you boys ride up. You want to look sharp then. Maverick and Tonto will stay with the horses. Link and me will start into the bank. You come in right behind us, Latch. Cherokee and Luther will stop at the corner. I want Scotty to drop across the side road in back of the horses and edge up to the main street. You'll see an old tar kettle there that they use for a waterin' trough, Scotty. Just plant yourself and drop behind it if things start to go wrong."

He told it off a second time so that there could be
no misunderstanding.

"When we git inside the bank Link and me will
line up whoever we find there. You git across the
counter, Latch, and git the money. Is that all plain
to yuh?"

They said it was. Bill passed two gunny sacks over
to Link.

"Latch will be the first one out of the bank," he
continued. "He'll go right to his horse. Link and me'll
back out after him. When we step out, Luther, you
and Cherokee can fall back to your horses. We'll pick
up Scotty at the corner. That side road runs south.
We'll take it even though it means crossin' the main
street. It may be pretty hot there for a few seconds."

They got away a minute later. Before they reached
the road Bill noticed that Six-gun was limping. The
others saw it too.

"Why, that horse is lame!" Link exclaimed.

"That's a break!" Luther fumed. "A horse goin'
lame at a time like this! I'm thinkin' Tas was right
when he said those claybanks was unlucky!"

"Nothin' to it!" Bill whipped back. "The horse
wasn't lame when I put him in the barn. He's picked
up a nail or a piece of glass."

He slipped out of his saddle anxiously and raised
Six-gun's right foreleg.

"Say, look at that!" he exclaimed. "It's a buckthorn! It ain't in deep enough to do any damage."

He got it out. The gelding seemed as sound as ever.

"Never heard of buckthorn this far north," Latch

declared as Bill held the thorn up for their inspection.

"Neither did I," he said. His voice was stony.

"You were lucky to get it out so soon," Cherokee drawled carelessly.

"I sure was," the red-haired one answered. "I'll just keep it for a little souvenir."

Chapter XV

IT LACKED a few minutes of three when they slid out of their saddles at the hitch-rack beside the bank. Scotty slipped across the street. Little Bill, Latch and Link walked briskly to the corner. Cherokee and Luther were only a step or two behind them.

Reed City was doing business as usual. Up and down the main street men and a sprinkling of women could be seen. Half a block away a little group lounged under the wooden awning of the hotel.

"This is workin' out nice," Bill muttered. He flicked a glance at Link. He wasn't worried about Latch. "Git your guns out as we step through the door," he said.

There were three men behind the counter. A fourth, a cowman, stood at the cashier's window. Not until Bill and the others were ten feet inside the door was the cashier or the others aware that three men with guns drawn had stepped into the bank.

"Stick 'em up!" Bill commanded hoarsely. "We got yuh covered!"

"Why—why it's Bill Stillings!" one of the three behind the counter gasped.

Bill saw that it was Monte Bassett who once had worked in the bank at Bowie. Monte's face was chalky with fright.

"It's me, all right, Monte! Just git your hands up and you won't git hurt!"

He was a bit taken back to find Bassett there. He had not seen him when he had stepped into the bank several days past. Still, it couldn't matter now that he was recognized.

The surprise of Monte and the bank officials was complete. Hands raised they started to back away.

"Freeze where you are!" Bill whipped out.

The man at the window turned as though to run. Link shoved a gun into his ribs. It took the fight out of him. Bill ran a hand over him and found a .44.

"Now you crawl over the counter with the others!" he jerked out. "Be foolish and you'll git all the trouble you want!"

The stranger obliged without delay.

Latch was in the cashier's cage already. The safe stood open. It did not take him long to scoop up everything in sight.

"Yuh ready?" Bill called to him.

"Yeh, we can be goin'," Latch answered.

They began to back out. They had not been in the bank more than three minutes. Not a shot had been fired. It had been almost too easy. And then as they reached the door their hearts missed a beat at the sight that greeted them. Coming down the main street was a herd of bawling steers that choked it from sidewalk to sidewalk.

The cattle were kicking up a great cloud of dust as they came on, heading for the railroad corrals.

"I thought we'd beat 'em across!" Luther ground

out. "There's a lot of 'em! We'll never get through! We'll have to go out the way we came in!"

Link groaned. Cherokee cursed.

"All right!" Bill snapped, refusing to lose his head. "Git to your horse, Latch! I'll fetch Scotty! Luther, you and Link and Cherokee cover us for a second!"

They realized that the street was deserted now. It had nothing to do with this herd of beef. Common sense told them their presence had been noted; that a whisper to the effect that the bank was being robbed had run over town with the speed of a prairie fire.

It was only a few steps to the corner of the bank building, but they had not yet reached it when someone pushed a rifle barrel out of the opening between the drug store and the saddlery shop opposite and began to work the trigger as rapidly as he could.

At the first blast Cherokee went down, rolled around on the sidewalk and jumped up quickly, the upper half of his right ear shot away.

"Git to your horses!" Little Bill cried. "I'll take care of that fellow!"

In such rapid succession that it did not seem possible that five shots could be fired from a single action gun, he stitched a little circle around the rifle opposite. Whether he hit the sniper or not, the firing ceased abruptly.

He took advantage of the lull and leaped around the corner of the building. Opposite him, Scotty was blazing away with both guns. He was a deadshot with a .44, and cool as ice now.

There wasn't a man in sight. For want of a better

target he smashed the old-fashioned street lamps to bits. The glass fell with a shivery sound and the oil streamed. For an instant a hat appeared on the roof of the drug store. He drilled a hole through it and it came sailing down into the street.

If anyone had to be impressed with the fact that this bunch could and would shoot they were being enlightened in a hurry.

The barking guns threw a panic into the oncoming steers. For an instant the leaders turned and tried to fight their way back through the herd. Failing in that, they lowered their heads, and bellowing with rage, dashed past the bank. The milling cattle began to streak after them. In a few seconds the whole herd was in mad motion.

"Come on!" Bill yelled at Scotty.

Together they backed to the horses. The others were mounted already. Cherokee was covered with blood. None of the others had got so much as a scratch. They had put away their six-guns and drawn their rifles from the scabbards.

It was down the side road now, doubling back on their own trail. They had not gone the distance of a city block, however, when they saw that several old wagons had been rolled out into the road. Suddenly from behind the barricade a dozen rifles began to erupt violently.

Bill pulled Six-gun up in the air and whirled him around before his forelegs hit the ground.

"We can't get through!" he shouted. "Follow me!"

Riding like a madman he dashed back to the main

street. The others were fanning it after him. A glance told him that none of them were down.

It seemed that he intended to fight his way through the herd. But at the last moment he sent the gelding tearing down the plank sidewalk.

He had to bend low to avoid the overhanging wooden awnings. His rifle was spurting flame, shattering windows and splintering store fronts. The others were at it too as they raced after him.

Through the biting swirl of gun smoke, rifles barking, glass crashing and steers bawling, they rode the length of the long block.

Finally they were around the herd. Open country beckoned ahead. In two or three minutes they had left the town behind.

They did not bother to look back; they knew they would be followed. Seconds were precious now.

Little Bill flashed a glance at the others.

"All here," he muttered.

Cherokee was a gory sight. Bill was not worried about him. The Kid was marked for life, but the wound was slight enough.

Three miles south of Reed City they topped a rise. At a signal from the red-haired one they pulled up to breathe their mounts. To the north a tiny dust cloud told them a posse had been organized and was after them.

"We're pretty far ahead of 'em," Link grinned.

"Yeh, they ain't breakin' their necks to overhaul us," Latch agreed. "We gave 'em a pretty good idee what to expect from us. I tell yuh, Bill, I've never seen neater work. You didn't miss a trick."

"Sure I did! I plumb overlooked the chance that we'd find that street blocked off for us with steers. We were just lucky, Latch."

"Just how lucky were we?" Cherokee demanded with a muttered curse.

"My guess would be between six and seven thousand," Latch answered. He took a good look at Cherokee. "I got to hand it to yuh, Kid," he laughed, "you're a ridin' massacre. Better let me tie up yore head."

"That'll have to wait," Bill spoke up. "We'll strike water later and clean it up right. You just got nicked. It can't be hurtin' yuh much."

"Not a bit," Cherokee sneered. "It's just one of them souvenirs you were talkin' about."

"That's the spirit!" Bill chuckled. "We both got one, Kid—only I'm carryin' mine around in my pocket."

Chapter XVI

THE Sawbuck wagon was creaking into Bowie again. Chalk Whipple sat on the seat in Maverick's place. The four men who rode ahead of the wagon with Tascosa were all new hands. The outfit was on its way north once more from another drive to the Nations, the Chickasaw country this time.

Seven weeks to a day had passed since the fight at Cain Springs.

Sam Swift sat under the wooden awning of the Bowie House, talking to Heck Short, the U. S. marshal, as the little outfit passed. Sam hailed Tascosa. His men went on, but the old man turned into the hitch-rail and climbed out of his saddle.

"Glad to see you, Tas," said Heck. "Take a chair and sit down!"

Short was a chunky man with the pink, unwrinkled cheeks of a child. His voice was strangely mild for a man of his formidable reputation. There were no notches in his guns—that was something he said he preferred to forget—but on the side of the law he had engaged in a hundred gun fights. His placid countenance suggested that he and Sam were only sitting there passing the time of day, for he was of that indomitable, bulldog breed of men who were slowly but surely bringing law and order to Oklahoma, and doing it without any flourish.

"Felt my ears burnin' as I rode in," Tascosa grinned. "You boys talkin' about me?"

"Talkin' about the bunch that used to draw their wages from you," said Sam. "They've just cracked a bank." He turned to Short for verification.

"No!" Tascosa shook his head forlornly. "Is that a fact, Heck?"

"Yeh, they rode into Reed City, across the Kansas line, day before yesterday in broad daylight, shot up the town and hoisted the bank. Apparently they made a clean get-away."

He supplied the details as he had heard them.

"That's too bad," Tas sighed. "I knew it was bound to happen. If a man is pushed outside the law there's nothin' for him to do but follow his trade. I know those boys is wild and reckless, but they were all square-shooters. I never found a wrong drop of blood in 'em."

Heck nodded. "I agree with you it's too bad," he said. "If they'd only held off I could have squared the trouble they had with Beaudry. The law's got a grudge against them now that can't be overlooked."

"Well, I'll say this for 'em," Sam volunteered, "when they get strong enough they'll do you a favor."

"How come?" Heck questioned.

"They'll wipe out the Sontags. With a bankroll and some reputation, Little Bill won't have any trouble buildin' up his gang."

"He's been doing that already," Short remarked

with a preoccupied air. "He had eight men in his bunch when he rode into Reed City."

They talked on for half an hour. Sam went down the street then. A few minutes later Tascosa got to his feet. He appeared his usual imperturbable self. Actually, life for him had lost its zest with the breaking up of the old Sawbuck outfit, a fact which he would have denied vehemently. It followed that the news he had just received was more disturbing than he let on.

"Don't be in a hurry," Heck murmured, motioning him back to his chair. "I want to talk to you."

"Private, yuh mean?"

The marshal nodded.

"Suppose we step inside," Tascosa suggested.

"No, I want to keep my eye on the sheriff's office. I've got some business with Beaudry."

Something in his tone said it was business of an unpleasant nature for Cash. Tascosa raised his eyebrows sharply and shot a glance across the street at the sheriff's office. Beaudry was apparently seated at his desk, for the crown of his hat was visible through the window.

"Yuh havin' some trouble with him?" he asked frankly.

"I don't expect to have very much trouble with him," Heck smiled. "I arrested Blackie Chilton, his chief deputy this mornin'."

"You did?" Tas gasped, unable to conceal his surprise.

"Yeh, I've got him chained to the safe down at the

depot right now. He's a federal prisoner and I'm taking him back to Guthrie tonight."

"Well, I do be damned!" the old man exclaimed.
"Have yuh got a real case against him, Heck?"

"Air tight." The marshal crossed his legs to a more
comfortable position. "When I came over here on that
Rock Island stick-up, I recognized Chilton . . . You've
heard of Black-faced Charlie, haven't you?"

"Him that used to run with Smoke and the old Wild
Bunch before there was a Sontag gang?"

"They're the same," said Heck. "I've been spending
a lot of time around Bowie the past weeks. I gave out
that it was the Rock Island job had me here; I've
really been watching Chilton and Beaudry. It's getting
pretty close to home when the chief deputy of a man
who has been suspected right and left of being hand
in glove with the Sontags turns out to be a proven
outlaw and the former running-mate of Smoke himself."

"I should think it was!" Tascosa bit savagely into
his plug of Honey Dew. "You're gittin' somewhere
now, Heck. Did that lizard make a break that told
you anythin'?"

"No, he didn't, Tas; but I've been making a little
headway just the same. I found out that he knew the
money was coming through on Number Nine that
night. Somebody sent him a mysterious telegram the
previous day; I got a copy of it."

"Then it *was* Beaudry who tipped off the Sontags!
Bill said it was!" Tas slapped his leg a whack to better

express his satisfaction. "What's he got to say about you arrestin' Chilton?"

"He hasn't said a word up to now. I've been sitting here for an hour, waiting for him to step over and have his say."

"Mebbe he'd prefer to do his talkin' in his own office," Tas suggested.

"Maybe," Heck smiled. "Suppose we walk over and hear what he has on his mind."

On crossing the road they found Beaudry's door locked. They exchanged a glance of mild surprise. Heck used his fist in a sharp knock. It brought no answer.

"He must be in there," Tas said. "I could see him from the porch." He tried to peer through the window but it was a foot or so too high for him from where he stood. "Give him a yell," he suggested.

"No, let's try the back way," Heck said. "It's just a step."

"Why, dammit, ain't no one here!" Tascosa exclaimed as they came through the rear door. "Looks like a cyclone had hit this place!"

Papers littered the floor. The drawers of Beaudry's desk stood pulled out, looking as though they had been rifled hurriedly. Short's only comment was an amused grunt. Tas shot a keen glance at him.

"You don't seem surprised," he said. "What do yuh make of it, Heck?"

"I take it that Beaudry has said good-bye to Bowie."

"What?" Tas gasped. "You mean that?"

"That's exactly what I mean," Heck declared. "He evidently figured things were getting too hot for him." He walked over to where Cash's familiar Stetson stood propped up on a pile of books so that it could be seen from across the street. "That was kinda clever of him," he smiled.

His utter lack of disappointment in finding that Beaudry had flown puzzled old Tas.

"Mebbe I'm thick," he grumbled, "but you sound as though you'd expected to find him gone."

"I hoped I would," Heck corrected. "I sure gave him every chance to get away."

"Mebbe that makes sense, but I don't git it," the old man got out crustily.

"Perhaps I can explain," Short smiled. "You know that it's only the guilty who run. I had the goods on Beaudry. It might have taken me a long time to prove it though. As sheriff of the county he could use his official position to slow me up in a number of ways. I've got him out on the end of a limb now."

"You may find it's a pretty long one before you git him to drop into your basket," Tascosa argued pessimistically. "Sure as fate he won't stop runnin' until he joins up with Smoke's bunch."

"I hope so," the marshal said with feeling. "It will answer a question or two that have been worrying me for the past few weeks."

He didn't offer to say what they were. For a few minutes he examined the litter on the floor and in the desk. Tascosa dropped into a chair and watched him for a while.

"I reckon it won't be no blow to this county to learn that the office of sheriff is vacant," he said heavily. "Mebbe it'll teach folks that if they won't take time to bother with votin', that a few blacklegs can soon git the run of things."

"There's something in that all right," Short agreed absent-mindedly as he closed the desk drawers. "I'll come back and look this stuff over later. The thing to do now is to drop into the courthouse and tell the county commissioners what's happened."

"Yeah," Tascosa muttered bitterly. "It won't take them no time to appoint someone to the job, but they'll never undo the damage Beaudry did. I tell yuh, Heck, it makes my blood boil when I think of them boys of mine bein' pushed outside the law by that skunk. Now they're robbin' banks. One job will lead to another."

"I know it," Heck acknowledged with deep concern. "It's as mean a thing as I ever heard of. Worst of it is, nothing can be done about it now. You know what the Kansas courts are. If they gave themselves up and made restitution they wouldn't get off with less than five years apiece. I know Bill would never listen to that. As long as he figures he's got something to square he'll never let anything get in the way of it."

The news that Beaudry had flown quite overshadowed word of the robbery at Reed City. It might not have been the case had Bowie suspected that Little Bill and his long riders were within fifteen miles of town at the time. Unmolested, they had crossed the Cimarron and were moving up the valley of the Skull.

As the afternoon began to wane they came in sight of the old Texas trail. Their horses were weary. Even the big gelding had a jaded look.

"We better pull up," Bill suggested. "We got water and grass here, and it's just as safe as any place we'll hit before dark."

The others were willing enough to climb out of their saddles. Several hours back they had butchered a yearling steer. Luther gathered wood and started a fire as Maverick cut thick steaks from the hindquarter of beef he had packed for miles.

"It was just seven weeks ago that we changed our minds about stayin' the night here," Link volunteered. "Things have changed considerable with us since then."

"They sure have," Little Bill murmured. Unconsciously his tone was sad. In common with the rest his face had a strained, gaunt look. In forty-eight hours they had not tasted a morsel of food. For a moment or two he gazed at the overcast sky.

"Goin' to rain," Scotty declared.

"Yeh, and blow too," Bill observed. "This slope in back of us has quite an overhang in places. We'll eat and then move up where we can be dry and comfortable. If it don't rain too long we'll wait it out here."

"You been right so far; I hope you ain't wrong now," Cherokee grumbled. Latch had put a tobacco poultice on his injured ear. It seemed to be having the desired effect.

They could hardly contain themselves as the appetizing odors from the fire began to assail their nostrils.

For once it was not necessary for Maverick to tell them to come and get it.

While they ate, the skies darkened ominously. The horses began to raise their heads nervously.

"This may be a twister," said Latch. "It looks pritty bad, off there to the west."

"I don't like the way she's coolin' off so sudden," Bill acknowledged.

The tree tops were beginning to thresh in the rising gale. Before they had finished eating, it was spitting rain.

"If we're goin' up the slope we better be about it," Luther urged. "That pocket right above us is cut back pretty deep. We won't find a better place."

"Reckon not," Bill agreed. "We'll take the horses up too and hobble 'em. We'll have to keep our eye on 'em if this storm breaks as bad as it looks."

The wind was blowing a gale by the time they reached the pocket, which they found to be big enough to afford shelter for their horses as well as themselves.

In a few seconds the rain began to drive down in sheets. They were warm and dry, however, and they soon had the air blue with the pleasant haze of tobacco smoke.

Their retreat was high enough to give them a commanding view of the country to the south and west on a clear day, but with the storm closing down on them like an opaque blanket their field of vision narrowed until they could see only several hundred yards beyond the creek.

Latch lay sprawled out beside Bill, watching the

play of lightning about them. Once or twice it struck uncomfortably close.

"It's a freak storm," Latch mused aloud. "Lightnin' ain't clearin' the air a bit."

Bill didn't answer. Latch glanced at him and saw that he was staring at something off beyond the creek. He tried to follow his gaze and saw a black, funnel-shaped cloud racing toward them at express-train speed. He expressed his surprise in a long-drawn whistle that brought the others to attention.

"There's hell and high water for someone!" he exclaimed shrilly. "She'll blow your freckles off when she tears up this creek! If that ain't a twister I never——"

"Latch," Bill interrupted, "do you see what I do— out there beyond the creek half a mile or so? Ain't that a herd of steers comin' up the old trail?"

"Wal, it sure is! That outfit must know they're in fer it the way they're hazin' 'em along. Watch the whole bunch stampede when that twister slashes through here!"

"They're bad off, sure enough!" Luther got out soberly. "I don't know what outfit it is. They seem to have four or five men."

"Whoever they are they know their business," Link declared. "They're tryin' to make the creek bottom. I hope they make it. It's goin' to be close."

Scotty and Tonto echoed his thought. In the excitement of the moment they were forgetting that they were no longer cowboys. It remained for Cherokee to remind them of it.

"Are the bunch of yuh losin' your wits?" he snarled

at them. "What do yuh mean, you hope they'll make this creek bottom? You better pull yourselves together! If you've got any worryin' to do, do it about our own outfit!"

"That's one way of lookin' at it," Bill answered him. "But men trailin' beef don't mean us no harm. If they makes the bottoms and hold that herd right below they'll do their damnedest not to see anythin' they shouldn't. I've been on both sides of the fence in a situation like this and I know what I'm talkin' about."

The Kid was silenced, though his glance was murderous.

Ignoring him, they turned to stare fixedly at the funnel of destruction that must tear a wide swath down the valley in another few seconds. It had grown so dark that night seemed to be closing down. The air was charged with electricity.

The little cow outfit below had reached the bend where, weeks past, Tascosa had hoped to find a way of getting his wagon down to the creek. It promised some protection from the tornado, if they could move down fast enough.

Suddenly it was so black they lost sight of the cattle altogether. With a wild, soprano scream the twister struck. Trees rocketed into the air. The dead brush and debris left behind by previous storms shot into the sky. Down along the stream itself the green willows were being slashed off as though some super-giant were wielding a mighty scythe. Boulders the size of a man's hand rained down on the little pocket on the slope. The eight men had all they could do to hold the snorting, panic-stricken horses. The little valley of the Skull was being scoured clean and made over, and in the bedlam of violence, of crackling lightning and crashing trees, of thudding boulders, they caught the bellowing of fear-crazed cattle.

The tornado was only a few seconds in venting its real venom. As it passed down the creek the skies lightened. The Skull was over its banks. Below them the old channel was so blocked with brush and down timber that it was making a new course.

It was not the ravages of the storm, however, that claimed their attention. They were looking for the outfit that had been caught on the bottoms. Scotty was the first to locate it.

"There's their wagon—pitched over just below the trail!" He pointed it out. "The horses are gone——"

"So are their steers!" Bill cried. "Look at 'em! They're high-tailin' it up the creek, hell bent for election! Those boys ain't got a chance of roundin' 'em up!"

"They sure ain't!" Luther agreed.

Little Bill's mouth tightened as he made a sudden decision. "Boys, I'm for givin' 'em a hand!"

There was an instant response from the others, with the exception of Cherokee.

"Say, this ain't none of our put in!" he burst out angrily.

"It won't hurt us none," Latch growled back at him. "It may make us some friends, and in this business yuh never know when you're goin' to need one."

"That may be," the Kid retorted, "but I don't want none of it!"

Little Bill whirled on him furiously, every inch of him bristling.

"Cherokee, you been gettin' under my hide all day!" he rasped. "I'm givin' the orders here. I said we was givin' these boys a hand. I'm sayin' it again—and I ain't tellin' yuh a third time! . . ."

Their eyes struck fire as they faced each other. For a moment anything was possible. The Kid shrugged his shoulders then and turned away with a sneering laugh.

"All right, you're boss, Bill," he muttered. "I only hope you don't find those gents are a rustlin' bunch that ain't lookin' for help."

Chapter XVII

THE rain continued to fall in torrents as they left the pocket. To save time they went on up the slope to the rim of the valley, intent on cutting across to the other side of the horseshoe bend the Skull described just above the old trail. Bill believed they could take the short cut and drop down to the bottoms again well in advance of the stampeding cattle.

Their horses found the footing slippery and treacherous until they reached the rim. It consumed precious seconds.

"Come on, we got to shake it up now!" Bill shouted. "We can make short work of this if we hurry!"

He was off in a swinging gallop. Without looking back he led the way across the plateau. It was not more than half a mile from one side of the bend to the other. Riding hard, heads lowered against the driving rain, they were soon across. In a slithering stop they pulled up in the sticky red clay to scan the bottoms below.

"We're here in time!" Luther called out. "No sight of 'em yet!"

Before they were halfway down to the creek, however, the stampeding herd hove in sight. Warming to the thrill of an old experience, they spread out fan-wise and with a wild halloo dashed at the charging steers.

Shouting, emptying their six-guns harmlessly over the heads of the cattle they literally stood them on their ears. The leaders turned back. In a few minutes the entire herd was milling.

Little Bill had but to catch sight of the brand they wore to know whose outfit this was.

"It's Leach Lytell's Two Bar O!" he ground out savagely. He had once worked for Lytell, and he had small cause to be doing him a favor.

Luther had recognized the brand too.

"It's Lytell's stuff!" he shouted across to Bill. "That ought to tickle yuh! If you've had enough, say so!"

"No, we'll see it through now!" Bill yelled back. "Just keep those critters millin' a little! We've got 'em bottled up if Lytell's men are on the job!"

It was some time before the cattle began to quiet down. Gradually, however, their panic passed and they began to drift back toward the trail.

From downstream a rider appeared. It was Lytell himself.

"Wal," he cried, "so it's your bunch, Bill! I was jest wonderin' who I had to thank." He was a heavy-set, sullen-faced man with little gimlet eyes. He pulled up a few feet from where Bill waited. "I'm obliged to yuh," he said curtly.

"You don't have to spread yourself any on my account," Bill told him. "A little mud and a good wettin' never hurt no one. If you've got these steers in hand we'll be movin' along."

"Mebbe you better," Lytell laughed hoarsely. "I hear you been keepin' pritty much on the move of late. Can't understand how you found time to tend to another man's business today."

"Say, what is this?" Latch flamed as he sent his horse in between the two men. "This is yore argyment, Bill, but this rat-eyed weasel don't seem to understand that we jest saved him a day's work, to say nothin' of his beef. I'm thinkin' it would be a good idee to slap some of the sass outa him." He fixed his watery eyes on Lytell. "I'd sure welcome the opportunity."

"Don't bother, Latch," Bill muttered. "I know this nombre. I worked for him once; did two men's work and got half the pay one ought to git, and when I pull up with a busted leg he tells me I'm through; that he ain't payin' wages to cripples. I always figgered I'd get even with you, Lytell, for that."

"I admire your way of doin' it," Cherokee said with a mocking laugh. "Why don't you ask him to apologize?"

The red-haired one withheld the retort that trembled on his tongue as one of Lytell's men rode up, an air of excitement on him.

"Lytell, we've just found Paint!" the newcomer exclaimed. "He's bad hurt!"

"Paint?" Bill echoed sharply. "What Paint is that?"

"Why, Paint Johnson, of Bowie!" the man informed him. "His horse went down when that twister struck and rolled on him. Before he could git up a steer gored him!"

Bill drew in his breath sharply and stiffened in his

saddle. The old Sawbuck men understood why—or believed they did, having only to recall that although Paint and Little Bill had long been rivals for Martha Southard's hand that it had never broken their friendship.

They were only partly right. For the moment Bill's thought was entirely of Martha, of the blow that disaster to Paint would be to her.

"She don't deserve to have anythin' like this come along on top of the misery I've made her," he told himself.

Leach Lytell, ignoring the open hostility evident in every eye, was raging violently at losing a man at this inopportune moment.

"Damn the careless fool!" he cursed. "Why'n't he look what he was doin'? Now we *are* short-handed!"

"You've been short-handed for years," Bill muttered contemptuously. "That ain't no accident with you." He swung around to Lytell's puncher. "Where's Paint at now?"

"'Bout halfway between here and the trail. I'm afraid to move him."

"You lead the way," Bill snapped at him. "Get us there in a hurry!"

"Say, wait a minute!" Lytell thundered. "If the bunch of you go chasin' down this creek you'll git my stuff runnin' ag'in!"

"To hell with you and your stuff!" Bill rifled back. "You've got a man down—bad hurt—and he happens to be a friend of mine!"

He and the others were thirty yards away before

Lytell heeled his horse and took after them, sputtering wrathfully.

They found Paint lying on the ground. He was covered with mud. It was even in his black, curly hair. He opened his eyes as Bill bent over him.

"Why, Bill," he murmured incredulously, "I didn't expect to see you here. Luther's here too, and the others——"

"Yeh, we're all here, Paint. It don't matter about that. I hear you're hurt pretty bad. Where did that steer git yuh?"

"In the right groin . . . I guess it's bad enough."

Bill beckoned to Latch.

"You're pretty handy about these things," he said. "I want you to take a look at it, Latch, and tell me what we can do."

"I'll have a look at it too!" Lytell bellowed as he pushed through the circle of men.

"Git back, and keep your lip buttoned!" Bill jerked out threateningly. "You see that he does, Link! Bend a gun over him if yuh have to!"

Lytell would have argued the matter, but Link hit him a clip on the jaw that shook a little sense into him.

Latch got to his feet after examining the wound and motioned for Bill to step aside with him.

"Ain't nothin' I kin do fer this boy but wash the dirt out and try to stop the blood a little," he said soberly. "He's goin' to die if he don't git to a doctor. Ain't no time to be lost about it either."

"I was afraid it was that-a-way," Bill muttered bleakly. He mulled it over for a moment. "You git busy, Latch, and do your best. If there's a chance for him I'll see that he gits it. They got a wagon here."

As Latch went back to Paint, Bill signaled for the others to step over to him. He told them what Latch had said.

"That's tough," Luther murmured. "What do yuh aim to do?"

"I aim to do all I can," Bill replied. "I want a couple of yuh to round up Lytell's team. In the meantime, some more of yuh can git your ropes on that wagon and right it. When you git it hitched, drive up here."

"You can't take my wagon that-a-way!" Lytell cried defiantly.

"We're takin' it!" Bill repeated. "Push him along with yuh, Link, and make him git his stuff out of it! It's a long way to Bowie—and Paint won't git no better on the way—but we'll see that he gits there."

"Bill, are yuh crazy?" Luther demanded. "If we ride into Bowie tonight we'll need more'n a doctor to help us!"

"I'm goin' in alone," Bill answered slowly. "I'll be there about nine o'clock."

"Yuh can't do it, Bill!" Link exclaimed excitedly. "It's foolish to even think of it!"

"You'll stub your toe, sure as shootin'!" Tonto agreed.

"That's right!" Luther echoed. "Why overplay your hand?"

Maverick and Scotty voiced similar sentiments. For once, Cherokee had no objection to raise.

"I don't know what you all are gettin' so excited about," he said. "He don't have to ride down the main street. I'm willin' to go in with him. Is that agreeable to you, Bill?"

The offer came unexpectedly, but Little Bill met it without lifting an eyelash. "That *would* be overplayin' my hand," he thought. His expression inscrutable, he glanced at the Kid. "No need of that, Cherokee," he said, "I'll be safer by myself."

If the Kid caught the double significance of the words, he dissembled it perfectly.

Even though Luther and the rest realized the futility of further argument they would have continued to object to Bill's going had he not ordered them to be on their way. As they went down the creek, he walked over to where Paint lay. He had not dismissed Cherokee from his mind.

"I can't figger out his play, unless all this talk about his breakin' with Beaudry was a bluff," he thought. "Wouldn't be no other way he could turn me up without gettin' himself snagged."

Paint was resting easier. Bill asked Latch to leave them alone for a moment. The rain had become a fine drizzle.

"You're takin' an awful chance in doin' this, Bill," Paint said when he had been told he was to be hurried to town.

"Well, it's me that's takin' it," Bill said grimly. "I owe this much to Martha. . . . I know she's mighty fond of you."

"Aw, I didn't have a chance when you were around," Paint insisted. His face was bloodless.

"I ain't around no more. . . . That's all over. You've got everythin' your way now."

"I don't want things that way," Paint scowled. "I just took this job with Lytell so I could keep out of Bowie until you were around again. I'll fight you fair for Martha. You ought to know it."

"I do," Bill murmured, looking away. "That's the only thing about this that's right, Paint. . . . I always said I wanted you to have her if I couldn't." With an effort he threw off his moodiness. "It's a long, joltin' ride into town. You'll have to buck up for it. It'll take about all you've got to make it."

Latch saw the Two Bar O wagon coming up the creek. Link was driving the team. Lytell was up beside him.

"Is that gent takin' this boy to town?" Latch asked.

"No, I'm takin' him," Bill answered. He explained briefly. Latch shook his head dubiously.

"You know your reasons," he said. "If you say you'll go, you'll go. You're almost certain to find trouble awaitin' yuh if this gent Lytell can arrange it."

"I want you to keep your eye on him, Latch. Don't let him pull away from the Skull till least an hour after dark."

"Yuh want us to linger here then?"

"Nothin' else to do," Bill said. "I don't figger you'll have any trouble unless he makes it for yuh."

"I'll undertake to gentle him if he starts anythin'," Latch grinned brazenly.

As gently as they could they placed Paint in the wagon on a bed of hay.

"You'll find this stuff waitin' for yuh when you hit Bowie," he told Lytell.

"I better find it! I'll settle your hash for this some day!"

Bill didn't bother to answer. Leading Six-gun around to the rear of the wagon he ran the bridle reins through the ring in the end-gate and knotted them. He was ready to leave, save for a word to his men. He walked aside with them beyond Lytell's hearing. After repeating what he had previously said to Latch, he added:

"If there's any orders necessary, Luther will give 'em. After yuh leave here tonight go right on as we planned. I'll meet you about noon tomorrow in the Witch Hills. You wait there for me. If I don't show up by evenin'—go on; you'll know I ain't comin'."

That was all he had to tell them. Without any formal leave-taking, he climbed up on the wagon and gathered up the reins.

"Luther, maybe you better follow me as far as the trail. It's pretty sticky there; you may have to put a rope on the wagon and snub me up a little."

Luther followed readily enough. The wagon rolled up the slope to the trail without any help from him however.

"It ain't bad here," he said.

"Course it ain't," Bill admitted. "I just wanted to say a last word to yuh: keep your eye on Cherokee. Don't let him have anythin' to say to Lytell that you don't hear. I don't want yuh to lose sight of him for a second."

Luther pulled down the corners of his mouth in a flinty stare.

"See here, Bill," he said fiercely, "are you holdin' back somethin'? If that double-crossin' coyote is makin' a move to sell us out, I want to know it!"

"He ain't had a chance to make a move," Bill replied, "and I ain't givin' him one."

"But you're as suspicious of him as ever——"

"I'm ten times as suspicious of him as I was the day Latch brought him into our fire."

"Then why don't we kick him out?"

Bill shook his head.

"Not yet, Luther. Cherokee's goin' to figger awful important in my plans later on."

Chapter XVIII

THE stars were out when Bill brought the jolting, springless wagon to a stop at Cain Springs. He had put two-thirds of the long ride behind them. Paint had not whimpered once. A score of times and more Bill had glanced back at him, wondering if life had flickered out.

"Yuh makin' it all right, Paint?" he queried now. "We've just pulled into the springs."

"I'm hanging on pretty well," Paint answered. "Get me a drink, will you? I'm terribly thirsty."

"You can't have no water, Paint. Worst thing in the world when you got somethin' wrong with your innards. I'll give the team a drop and we'll be movin' along."

He knew the boy was suffering untold torture. He offered to roll him a cigarette, but Paint said no.

The springs had not changed since Bill had seen them last. The old stone house and the trough prompted old memories. He had no time for them tonight.

The horses were too warm to be given much water. They quickly guzzled up what little he offered them.

"We'll be in Bowie in less than two hours," he told

Paint as they started on again. "Just lay quiet and don't try to talk."

Since leaving the Skull they had seen no one. Several miles north of Cain Springs, however, Bill saw a freighting outfit creeping toward them. There had been no rain here, and the eight-mule team was kicking up clouds of dust. The skinner was perched high on his load, swaying back and forth with the roll of the wagon and warbling to himself.

As they drew abreast, the freighter pulled up and hailed Bill. Courtesy of the country demanded that he stop too. Instead, he turned loose a flood of unintelligible Spanish and drove on.

"The hell yuh say!" the freighter yelled back. Deciding that he had been offended, he got to his feet groggily and made the air smoke with his cursing. Bill grinned to himself and whipped up the team.

"I can see the lights of Bowie," he announced to Paint an hour later. "We ain't very far out now."

Danger to himself began here. Both of them realized it.

"Bill—just leave me in the wagon at the edge of town," Paint murmured weakly. "Someone will pass and find me."

"No, I'll take you in myself," Bill demurred. "A few minutes may mean a lot to you. I'll go across the flats and swing around by Lew Brown's feed barn. If there ain't no one in sight I'll drive right into the Southards' backyard."

It was quite the usual thing for men to camp out on the flat. Several wagons were there tonight. Bill kept away from them and passed the old feed barn without even being hailed.

He was right in town now. Off to his left he could see down the main street. Presently he reached the road that led to the Rock Island depot. It ran at a right angle to the main street. He had to cross it to reach Doc Southard's house.

"I'm goin' right across," he decided. "It'll be better than pullin' up here and waitin' to size things up."

He was halfway over the side road when two men rounded the corner from the main street, a block away. Who they were, or what business they had there, he could not tell. Without urging the team to move faster he rolled into the Southard yard.

The two men were passing now. They glanced in his direction, and for a moment he thought they were going to stop. They went on, however, and he began to breathe easier.

"We're here," he told Paint. "I'll go to the door and call Doc. . . . I'll be gittin' along then. I—I hope yuh make it all right——"

"If I do I'll never forget what you did, Bill. . . . Take care of yourself——"

Leading the big gelding, Bill approached the front door. Lights glowed within. At this hour Martha would be home.

"I hope it ain't her who comes out," he sighed. "I want to git away without her seein' me."

In answer to his knock someone approached the door. It was not Martha's buoyant step. The next moment, to his surprise, he found Tascosa facing him.

"Well for——" Tas started to exclaim.

"Shut the door and step out here," Bill cut him off.

His tone was so tense it commanded obedience. His eyes large with questions, Tascosa followed him out.

"Is Doc home?"

"Why, yes——" Tas answered. "Is it to see Doc that you take a chance of runnin' into town like this?"

Bill told him why he was there. Tas shook his head pityingly as he heard him out, and his sympathy was as much for Bill as Paint.

"Yo're a precious damn fool, doin' a thing like this!" he groaned. "What can yuh be thinkin' of? Do yuh know Heck Short is in Bowie? I bet he's within two blocks of yuh this second!"

The news was not without effect on Little Bill.

"I'll keep out of his way," he muttered. "You know why I had to come. Let it go at that. You and Doc git this boy in the house!"

He put a hand on his saddle horn, ready to go.

"Jest a minute," Tas insisted. "Did yuh hear what happened in Bowie today? About Chilton and Beaudry, I mean."

"Why, no——"

"It'll interest yuh," Tas promised. "Heck arrested Chilton this mornin'. Some time later Beaudry disappeared."

Bill soon had the facts out of him. He did not try to hide his satisfaction.

"Kin Lamb has been appointed to fill out Beaudry's term," Tas went on. "It's goin' to be unhealthy fer a lot of yuh around here, the way things is goin'. They're movin' fast, Bill."

"They'll be movin' a lot faster directly," the red-haired one scowled.

Behind them the door opened. Through the branches of the sycamore under which they stood, Bill saw Martha. His throat tightened as he beheld her.

"Tas—where are you?" she called.

Bill clutched the old man's arm. "Don't let her know I'm here!" he whispered huskily.

"You call your pa, Martha," Tascosa answered her. "There's a man here needs a doctor."

She left the door at once to notify her father. Since childhood she had become used to having sick and wounded men brought to their door at all times of the day and night.

His face stony, Little Bill vaulted into his saddle.

"Yo're makin' a mistake," Tas upbraided him. "You shouldn't go without seein' her. Yuh may never git another chance."

"Don't I know it!" Bill groaned. "Ain't that the best reason in the world why I shouldn't see her to-night?"

"She often speaks of yuh," Tas persisted. "What you've done ain't turned her ag'in yuh."

"It will sooner or later. No use denyin' the truth: I'm outside the law, and my life is goin' to be lived among outlaws, doin' as they do. That means goin' from bad to worse. I don't want her to remember me. Let her forget she ever knew anybody by the name of Bill Stillings."

Without waiting for Tascosa to speak he swung the gelding around and rode away. He was in a mood to dare anything. Before he was halfway across the flats he changed his course suddenly and headed for the depot, his brain afire with the wild, utterly reckless idea of kidnapping Blackie Chilton and forcing him to confess who had killed Waco.

The Guthrie train was not due for almost an hour. There might be one or two sleepy-eyed travelers in the waiting-room. The ticket window would not be open, however. He could walk through the waiting-room and into the office without being seen by the agent or night operator until he opened the office door. They didn't figure to make him any trouble when they found a gun leveled at them. If Heck Short had only a leg chain on Chilton it would be no trick to shoot off the lock.

The tracks lay between him and the depot. At the last moment some sense of caution returned to him and he changed his mind about riding up boldly. Half a dozen stock cars stood on the siding. Leaving his horse in the brush, he stole across the tracks and climbed to the top of an empty car. On hands and knees he proceeded from one to the other until he could look into the depot.

He took one look and dropped back out of sight. Three men lounged just inside the door. Ten yards away, in the shadow of the baggage room he caught the glow of three or four cigarettes.

He thought he had recognized one of the three men in the waiting-room. He peered over a second time.

There was no room for doubt now. The man nearest the door was Grat Sontag.

"They're here to take Chilton away from Short!" he told himself as he flattened down on the car. "There's seven or eight of 'em!"

Thought of the jack-pot he had almost walked into sent a little shiver down his spine. He lay there for a second or two, trying to decide whether to shoot it out with them or steal away unobserved.

According to his code it was murder to shoot a man down without warning, and that held whether the man deserved killing or not. That meant giving away the advantage that was now his. Even so he did not doubt that he could pick off one or two of them.

"I could hold off the others for a few minutes," he said to himself, "but it wouldn't work out for me. Before I got through with 'em, Short and this new sheriff would have me surrounded. The thing for me to do is to git out of here."

A freight engine clanked past the depot. A brakeman ran ahead and threw a switch to let it in on the siding. The empties were being shunted down to the railroad corrals. Bill let himself be carried down the tracks for a hundred yards before he swung off and made his way back to his horse.

He'd had time to think things over and he retraced his way to town, passing within a few yards of the spot where he had left Tascosa. He continued on until he was within a block of the hotel. Turning into an alley then that ran between the Bowie Mercantile Company and another store he reached the main street. Leaving his horse at the hitch-rack, he stepped back into the alley. He knew Short must pass him on his way to the depot, and he settled back to wait for him.

Maybe fifteen minutes passed before he saw the marshal leave the hotel and start up the street.

Heck came along with unhurried step. As he reached the entrance to the alley Bill threw a gun on him.

"Don't you move!" he commanded. "I've got you covered, Heck!"

"Well," Short exclaimed on recognizing him, "you're coming pretty fast, Bill, walking right into Bowie and sticking me up."

"This ain't a stick-up, Heck. I'm here to do yuh a favor, but don't you make a move for your guns."

"I'm listening," Short said calmly. "What is it?"

"Don't you walk into that depot alone! Grat and a bunch are there! They're waitin' to take Chilton away from yuh."

"Well, that *is* a favor." Short pursed his lips thoughtfully. There was little in his calm, unruffled manner to suggest that he was well aware that the warning he had just received had possibly saved his life. "Maybe I can do *you* a favor," he said softly. "I'll tell you who killed your father. . . . It was Cash Beaudry."

With another man, Bill would have taken it as a trick to throw him off his guard with surprise. Heck Short was above anything of that sort, the circumstances considered.

"So it was Beaudry!" Bill got out, his voice harder than chilled steel. "How long have yuh known it, Heck?—and how do yuh come to know it?"

"I wasn't positive until now," Short informed him. "I knew, though, the second you told me the Sontags had come for Chilton. I take it that you heard Beaudry shook the dust of this town off his feet this morning. He's been gone just long enough to get word to Smoke and give this bunch time to ride in here by crowding their broncs."

"I'd figgered that out," Bill said impatiently. "It ain't tellin' me what I want to know."

"I'll try it another way," Short ventured. "The night that Smoke stopped that Rock Island train your father stepped into the Longhorn Saloon here in Bowie. There was a bunch present—all congratulating him. Beaudry walked in. His talk was pretty loose. Among other things he told them that the package Smoke had got out of the safe was just a bundle of billheads for Hahn's butcher shop."

"I've heard that too—" Bill muttered.

"It was a bad slip up, Bill. I caught it soon enough. I talked to every man who'd spoken to your father from the time of the robbery until he stood there against the bar. He hadn't told a one of them what was in that package. Maybe he didn't know himself. Beaudry knew it though—and the only way he could have come by the information was because he was right there on the Skull with the Sontags when the package was opened."

"Say—pop told Chalk that Beaudry had given himself dead away," Bill exclaimed. "I never knew what he meant——"

"You know now," said Heck, "and you can take it for granted that Beaudry and Chilton realized that Waco had caught the slip. Now Smoke don't forgive a thing like that in a man. You can't be thick and string along with him. So it was up to Beaudry to do something in a hurry. . . . The next morning your father's mouth was closed forever."

Bill nodded to himself. "I see—" he whispered tensely. "You can't be wrong about it."

"There's no chance of my being wrong. If Beaudry didn't get your father, then Smoke did, and I'm telling you that if Beaudry had stalled, and it had been necessary for Smoke to come in and tend to the job, that you would have found two dead men in Bowie that morning."

"It's plain enough," Bill murmured.

"It is, now that I know where Beaudry lit out for today," Short agreed. "If he'd ever had words with Smoke he would have been afraid to show his face in the Strip."

The red-haired one nodded. The observation was so obviously true that he found any comment beside the point.

"I'm much obliged, Heck," he said simply. "Now if you'll just turn around and head back for the hotel I'll get out of town."

"Don't lose any time about it," Short replied brusquely. "I got to regard you as I would any other outlaw, Bill. It's war to the hilt between us; you know that. I'll pick you up the first chance I get."

Little Bill grinned. "When you come for me, come a smokin'," he said.

"That's the way I'll come." There was no mirth in the marshal's voice. "It ain't anything I look forward to with pleasure. You're playing a losing hand, Bill. Dead or alive I'll get you in the end, and it's a damned shame that it's so. But there's times when it's too late for advice. I know I'm just wasting my breath now."

Without another word he turned on his heels and strode up the street. When a hundred yards separated them, Little Bill forked his horse and rode away.

Chapter XIX

"THE afternoon's half gone and he ain't here yet," Luther muttered nervously as he scanned the country to the east for the hundredth time. "I'm thinkin' he won't be comin'."

He, Latch and Link had climbed to the crest of a hill. The others waited below. For nearly five hours they had waited at the rendezvous.

"He'll be along all right," said Latch. "You underestimate him, Luther; he's sharp as a whip."

"Yeh, and they're just the kind who overplay their hand," Luther returned gloomily.

"That's what I been thinkin'," Link seconded. "That Lytell is poison. If he was able to figger out a way of gettin' word to Bowie you can bet he did it."

"He would have been hours too late," Latch argued. "The two of you have been jumpy ever since Bill left us. I tell yuh this will work out. It wa'n't necessary to have any words with the Kid jest because he took it on himself to pump Lytell a little."

"I got a different idea about that," Luther growled. "I warned him not to have no talk with Lytell. I meant it. If he thinks I shut him up just to put the crawl on him he's crazy."

"Whatever he thinks he'll git over it," Link observed philosophically, shading his eyes with his hand as he stared intently at a moving speck to the northeast. "That's a man on horseback. I don't know whether it's Bill or not, but he's sure ridin' a long-legged critter that's gaited mighty like Six-gun."

Fifteen minutes passed before they agreed that it was Little Bill at last. They signaled to the others below that he was in sight and then started down the slope.

"I didn't mean to hold yuh up quite so long," the red-haired one remarked casually as he joined them. Hooking a leg over his saddle-horn he calmly proceeded to roll a cigarette.

"Ain't yuh goin' to give an account of yourself?" Luther asked impatiently. "We been here for hours."

"Yeh, I've sure got some news for yuh," Bill smiled. "Cash Beaudry has flown the coop; Blackie Chilton is on his way to Guthrie in irons and Kin Lamb is the new sheriff of Cimarron County——"

It pulled Cherokee to his feet, his eyes widened to circles of consternation. The others were hardly less excited.

"If you're givin' us facts, suppose you give us all of 'em!" the Kid got out tensely.

"Give me a chance," Bill drawled. Cherokee was reacting just as he had figured he would.

Save for their muttered expressions of astonishment and satisfaction they permitted Bill to tell his story without interruption. It was piling surprise upon surprise for him to proceed from his meeting with Tascosa to his encounter with Heck Short.

Instead of hurling a barrage of questions at him as he finished, they were silent for a moment, each busy with his own thoughts.

Luther was the first to find his tongue.

"So it was Beaudry that got pop, eh?" he muttered fiercely. "Well—that don't change nothin' for us, does it?"

"Not a thing!" Bill answered, his face hard in a flash. "Beaudry got him, but Smoke was responsible. They'll learn that I was in Bowie, and figger that I had somethin' to do with Heck bein' tipped off. They'll be comin' after us for sure now."

"What happened at the depot?" Cherokee asked. His face was inscrutable once more.

"Well, I pulled up out on the flats," Bill told him. "I figgered I'd hear some shootin', but not a shot was fired. A few minutes later Grat and his bunch fanned it west. Chilton wasn't with 'em."

"That's one out of the way then," the Kid said with satisfaction. His tone sounded surprisingly sincere, even to Bill. It didn't fit in at all with certain conclusions he had reached.

They camped in the Strip that night. Seated around the fire, Bill discussed their immediate future. Money was set aside to pay Reb Leflett, and another sum with which to outfit themselves. The balance was divided share for share.

"I suppose Reb can get the guns and stuff we need," Bill remarked. "But the fact is, I'd like to keep out of that country up there for a few weeks."

"Well, there's always Windy Ben to fall back on,"

said Latch. "You'll pay him a little more, but he'll have what we want. As for Reb—he won't mind waitin' for his money."

All of them were more or less familiar with old Ben. For years he had been moving about the Strip and Panhandle in his old yellow wagon. He pretended to be just a peddler of notions and odds and ends that men living in the open always needed. He was really a fence for the outlaw gangs.

"Can you locate him?" Bill inquired.

"Sure! He'll either be home on Hat Creek or between there and the Raton Peaks at this time of the month. He has to git pretty far west to do business with Doc Mundy's old crowd. If—" He broke off abruptly to turn something over in his mind that had just occurred to him. Pulling at his mustache, he fixed his eyes on Bill in a contemplative squint. "Speakin' o' Raton," he mused aloud, "reminds me o' sunthin'. If yuh think we'll be needin' an extra man or two right soon, I might look up Bitter Root and Flash Moffet. They were the backbone of the ole Mundy bunch, an' they ain't forgot what Smoke did to Doc. If yuh never hear o' them east o' the peaks no more it's only because they figger two or three don't stand no chance against the Sontags. If they knew a bunch was organizin', they'd come quick enough."

"Well, we sure could use 'em!" Bill exclaimed without hesitation. "I've heard enough about Bitter Root and Flash to know they'll do to take along no matter how tough the goin' gits. Suppose you and Scotty pull away from here at daybreak for Hat Creek. Do your business with old Ben and then look up Bitter Root and Flash. How long do yuh think you'll be gone?"

"Not more than three days, I'd say," Latch ventured. "Will we find yuh here when we git back?"

"No, you won't," Bill answered. "I was just gettin' around to that. Do yuh know a place on the Bowie road that some of the old-timers used to call Squaw Meadows?" He was speaking to all of them now.

Tonto seemed to be the only one who was not familiar with the Meadows.

"Well, there's an old sod shanty in there that ain't been occupied for three or four years," Bill continued. "That's where we're goin'. There's lumber enough around the place to build some bunks. We'll put our horses back in the brush where they can fatten up a little. As for ourselves, we'll keep out of sight pretty well. I stopped there this mornin' and had a look around. The place will suit us to a T."

Luther shook his head. Link and Latch objected too.

"That's too close to Bowie," said Luther.

"Ain't that the best reason why no one will be lookin' there for us?" Bill came back. "As for Kin Lamb, he ain't got no authority west of the county line."

"That ain't the case with Short," Link argued. "If Heck learns we're holed up there he'll be after us with a bunch of deputies."

"You're wrong," Bill insisted. "Heck may stumble onto us by accident, but he ain't likely to come at us with a posse for a showdown. Take it from me, he

knows where to find the Sontags, but he ain't ridin'
into the Grocery, and he won't be ridin' into the
Meadows. He's too cagy to do his fightin' in the Strip.
He's always got his ear to the ground, and when
there's a leak, he turns up awful sudden, like he did
when he cleaned out the Yeagers."

"I ain't disagreein' with yuh on that end of it,"
Latch declared, "but I'm thinkin' we won't be in the
Meadows very long before some Sontag spy locates
us. Of course, if you're ready for them, that's somethin' else."

"Well, we ain't ready for 'em," said Bill. Without
seeming to, he was watching the Kid. Cherokee had
not only said nothing but he pretended an utter lack
of interest in the conversation. It was such clumsy dissembling that it secretly amused Little Bill. "I ain't
goin' to be hurried into anythin' with them. If we lay
out quiet in the Meadows we can be there a long time
before Smoke tumbles to where we're at."

Other arguments were voiced against his plan, but
in the end he had his way. Before rolling up in their
blankets for the night, he and Luther went out to have
a look at the picketed horses. The animals were all
right.

"Bill, you're bein' headstrong about goin' to the
Meadows," Luther said as they turned back to their
smouldering fire. "You know damned well we won't
be there a week before Smoke is tipped off."

"Course I know it," his brother grinned. "That's
just why we're goin' there, Luther. I know more'n
I've been tellin'. I don't want the bunch to know yet—

especially the Kid—but my plans are all set. Comin'
out of Bowie I followed Grat. I know the trail they
use in goin' back and forth. It runs within a mile of
the shanty."

"Well, what's the idea?"

"Just this, Luther: I figger they'll soon enough discover where we are. But they won't know we ain't all
there. It ain't likely they'll make a move until they've
thought it over pretty thoroughly. Some mornin'
they'll surround the cabin and lay out for an hour or
two in the hope that they can pick off one or two of
us before they close in."

"Of course that's what they'll do!" Luther exclaimed hotly. "We'll be in a bad spot. They'll be
between us and our horses——"

"No, they won't," Bill assured him. "We're goin'
to be most awful sure just when we been located.
We'll stall around then only as long as we're dead sure
it's safe. By doin' a little spyin' on our own account
we'll know when the Sontags are comin' for us. If
things work out as I believe they will, we'll be headin'
for the Black Grocery at the very time they're headin'
this-a-way."

Luther expressed his surprise in a low whistle.

"So that's your scheme, eh?" he queried sharply.

"You've heard it! Smoke will take along about
every top man he's got when he goes to the Meadows.
That ought to make things pretty easy for us, especially if Latch comes back with Bitter Root and Flash.
We'll clean out that crowd. By the time Smoke's bunch
returns to the Grocery, we'll be ready for 'em."

"That's makin' 'em divide their forces all right," said Luther. "We couldn't ask for nothin' better. But just how are we goin' to ride into the Grocery?"

"Cherokee will take us in—or it'll be his last ride! No doubt in my mind but what he knows the ropes. If we have to go in without him, we'll try it from the west. There's some broken country in that direction. . . ."

"Yeh. . . ." Luther muttered. He had no suggestion to make. He was beginning to see that Latch was right; that he had never realized his brother's capacity for leadership. Bill had taken to this wild life with undreamed-of ability for doing the unexpected.

They talked on for a minute or two and then walked back to the fire.

"You take care of Smoke, Luther," Bill said with a preoccupied air. "I'll get Beaudry."

The following morning, soon after Latch and Scotty got away, the red-haired one led the others to the sod shanty in the Meadows. Arrived there, the horses were led to a green pasture below the shanty and hobbled. A man was told off to guard them.

During the years the crude house had stood idle it had fallen into bad repair. They were not minded to do anything about that. Building some makeshift bunks, they settled down to rest. That evening, Little Bill took all of them into his confidence.

It surprised them to learn that the showdown with the Sontags was so near. They adjusted themselves to it quickly enough. If there was any thought among them that they were striking too soon, that the issue should be put off for a week or month, it was not voiced. They seemed to feel that since they had a score to settle that now was as good a time as any—and that included Cherokee. He smoked his cigarette with great deliberation, and his black eyes were cold and calculating.

"From the mornin' on we'll ride a half-mile circle about the shanty," Bill told them. "Two men will go out at a time. You're likely to see someone. If you do, use your heads. With a little judgment you'll be able to decide whether it's somebody spyin' on us or a man just happenin' along on his way to Bowie. Cherokee and me will make the first swing around."

"I wish you'd take another man," the Kid spoke up. "This laig is hurtin' me plenty again. It's awful stiff."

It was the first time in days that he had mentioned his wounded leg.

"All right," Bill agreed readily. "Tonto can go with me. I want yuh to take care of yourself, Kid; I'll sure be needin' yuh in a day or two."

Long after the others were asleep, Little Bill lay in his bunk wondering what was behind Cherokee's reluctance to leave the shanty. He couldn't begin to understand it.

"Here's a chance made to order for him to double-cross us, and he walks away from it," he thought. "I sure figgered he'd break his neck to git word to Smoke."

He and Tonto were out until noon the following morning. They had not seen a soul. Link and Maverick went out that afternoon. The Kid still complained of his leg.

"Well, yuh're sure able to keep an eye on our broncs," Bill told him. "Yuh go down and spell Luther for a while."

The Kid did not object. Luther came in a few minutes later. There was a perplexed frown on his face.

"Yuh're takin' a chance, ain't yuh, sendin' Cherokee out by himself?" he asked his brother.

"I aim to keep an eye on him this afternoon," Bill assured him. "Maybe this is the openin' he's been anglin' for."

"Maybe," Luther muttered. "What do yuh make of the way he's actin'?"

Bill shrugged his shoulders. "I wish I knew. My guess is that he's hopin' to keep us out of a fight with the Sontags."

"The skunk!" Tonto growled. "There's been some talk about that geldin' of yourn bein' bad luck. I bet in the end you'll find the Injun is our bad luck."

"It may work out that-a-way," Bill answered moodily. "If it does, we can't ever say we didn't have our eyes open."

He watched the Kid that afternoon. Cherokee never made a suspicious move. Not for a minute did he leave the horse cavy. With his back propped against a rock, his hat pulled low over his eyes, he sat for hours in the deepest meditation.

"He sure acts like a man who don't know his own mind," Bill mused. "That may be just the case."

The success of his plans depended utterly on word

of their presence being conveyed to the Sontags. He had fully expected that the Kid would help to perform that service. Fortunately it did not depend solely on him.

"It may take longer, but they'll find out," Bill assured himself.

On the morning of their third day in the Meadows, he arose at sun-up fully expecting that Latch and Scotty would ride in before the morning was very far along. The day passed without bringing them. Nor did they come the following morning. The sun swung across the sky and the lengthening shadows of early evening marched down the distant hills, and still they did not come.

"What can be keepin' 'em?" Bill demanded in his growing anxiety. The others were asking themselves the same question. A hundred things could have happened to the two men. One guess was as good as another.

"They may be havin' some trouble locatin' old Ben," Cherokee observed. "I ain't worryin'——"

"I see yuh ain't!" Bill snapped at him. He could not help asking himself if the Kid could have stacked the deck against Latch and Scotty.

He was still pacing the floor when Luther and Maverick pulled up their mounts sharply at the door. There was an air of excitement about them.

"Well, they're keepin' cases on us!" Luther announced tensely. "We damn near stumbled over a man on the way in."

Bill's head went up with a jerk.

"He knows yuh saw him, eh?"

"We pretended not to," Luther answered. "After comin' on a way we turned back; he was hittin' only the high places in his hurry to get away."

"Say, that's goin' to complicate things for us, comin' right now," Link remarked. "Latch and Scotty not here yet. We can't be stallin' around much longer."

"We'll see what mornin' brings," Bill said thoughtfully.

Morning dawned, but the two men who had ridden west failed to appear.

"I'll give 'em till evenin'," Bill decided. "In the meantime, we'll take good care not to be jumped. Cherokee and me'll stay here; the rest of yuh keep movin' around the Meadows. Yuh can bring our horses in. If yuh see anythin' that looks queer, fire a shot and head for the shanty."

At five o'clock that afternoon, Little Bill told them they were going to move.

"Roll your blankets; it ain't safe to wait no longer."

A quarter of an hour later they were preparing to ride away when Luther caught a glimpse of four horsemen, off to the south.

"They're headin' straight for the shanty," he exclaimed. "It may be Latch and——"

"It's them, all right!" Bill interrupted, his voice shrill. "We'll ride out and meet 'em; I don't want to linger here another minute!"

Chapter XX

LITTLE BILL was the first to reach the four men.

"Git your broncs turned around and work back into the brush a ways!" he called out as he rode up to them. "The Meadows is gittin' too warm for us!"

He had never laid eyes on Bitter Root or Flash Moffet. He could not be sure even now that one of the two strangers who rode with Scotty and Latch was Flash, but there was no question in his mind concerning the other, a lean, hatchet-faced man, older even than Latch, whose legs were so long that his pony appeared grotesquely small for him.

In a few minutes they were out of sight of the shanty. Bill gave the signal to pull up.

"Well," he grinned, "yuh didn't come none too soon. We'd about given yuh up." He shifted around in his saddle to face the two strangers. "I don't have to be told that this is Bitter Root," he said, "but I'll have to make a guess that the other one of yuh is Flash Moffet."

"It's Flash, sure enough," Latch laughed. "We had some trouble locatin' him."

"You know how that is," Flash said, with a little chuckle. "There's times when it's advisable to make yourself awful scarce. . . . It didn't take us long to get here, once we got started. . . . Bitter Root and me have got some unfinished business in this neighborhood." His voice was suddenly bitter, even though he continued to smile.

"Now that's sure a fact," Bitter Root agreed. "The debt's bin runnin' along some time, but we bin keepin' account of the interest, and we're hopin' to collect in full this trip." His faded blue eyes had been shifting from one to the other, taking them all in. "You boys are all strangers to me, except this one," he ran on, his glance resting on Cherokee. "I seem to remember you awful well, for some reason."

"Yeh?" the Kid queried insolently.

"Yeh," Bitter Root echoed, and all the friendliness was gone from his tone. "You're the breed that used to rustle stuff along with Cash Beaudry and Little Arkansaw."

Cherokee's teeth flashed in a hideous grin. Few men had the temerity to call him a breed to his face. Bill fully expected to see him go for his guns. Certainly that was what the Kid longed to do; it was written all over his face. Something stayed his hand. Possibly it was Bitter Root's formidable reputation.

"Well, what about it?" he sneered.

"Not a thing," Bitter Root said quietly. "I've rustled a few steers myself in my time, but I was jest wonderin' if you wa'n't on the wrong side of the fence, ridin' with this bunch. All your old friends seem to git along pritty smooth with Smoke."

"I'm where I want to be," Cherokee informed him surlily.

"Jest be sure you are," Bitter Root muttered as he turned away. "It ain't no time for straddlin' the fence. Smoke and nigh a dozen men are headin' this way right now."

"Yuh mean you saw 'em?" Bill demanded sharply.

"I'll say we saw 'em!" Latch answered him. "They're movin' so cautious that they must have heard you were in the Meadows."

"That's fine! Everythin's workin' out just right." Bill's eyes were glowing. He had to explain the situation to the four men who had just joined them.

"That's foxin' 'em!" Bitter Root exclaimed. "We got your rifles and so forth here."

"I see yuh have," Bill replied. "Better let us git acquainted with 'em right off. We don't want to waste no more time here than we have to."

Just before night fell they reached the hidden spring where Latch and Cherokee had first joined them.

"We'll cache everythin' here," Bill ordered. "We want to ride as light as we can. I reckon it's safe to make a fire. We'll have a bite to eat, and later on we can be movin' along. The moon won't bother us much tonight."

He motioned for Bitter Root to follow him and started up the slope.

"We'll just have a look around," he said. "Be back in a few minutes.

They were soon out of sight of the camp.

"What about this Injun?" Bitter Root asked abruptly. "I pritty near know he's a double-crossin' rat. Latch thinks he's all right; you seem to think so too."

"Not for a second," Bill replied. "I figger he tried to lame my horse just as we were about to ride into Reed City. The other day on the Skull he did his damnedest to tie some trouble on me. So I ain't foolin' myself about him. I know him and Beaudry used to pal together. The talk is that they fell out some time back. I didn't know the two of 'em had ever run with Little Arkansaw."

"Wal, they did—for nigh on a year. I hear things— mebbe some talk that you don't. That breed and Beau- dry are as thick as they ever was. The only truth in the talk about their fallin' out came from the fact that Smoke turned his thumbs down on the Cherokee Kid, and he didn't do that because he knew the skunk would sell out the best man that ever lived. . . . Smoke's done a little of that himself."

"What was his reason?" Bill asked.

"Why, it goes back to Beaudry. That hombre is am- bitious." Bitter Root laughed contemptuously. "You won't believe it, but he's bin troubled for a long time with the idear that he'd put Smoke and Grat on the shelf some day and take things over himself———"

"And Cherokee was to be his right-hand man, eh?"

"Why, sure! But Smoke spiked that. No doubt the Injun hates him, but you know how a breed hangs onto an idear when he gits it. Take it from me, he ain't quit thinkin' for a minute that him and Cash won't turn the trick some day."

"Well, that answers some things that have had me puzzled," Bill muttered. He shook his head to himself as he began to understand why Cherokee had made no attempt to communicate with the Sontags while he was in the Meadows. He mentioned the matter to Bitter Root.

"He *was* in sunthin' of a fix, wa'n't he?" Bitter Root chuckled scornfully. "He was dead willin' to have Smoke and Grat knocked off, but he knew Beaudry was at the Grocery, and he didn't want anythin' to come off that might rub Cash out."

"Well, Beaudry ain't there now," said Bill. "It's a sure bet he's ridin' with Smoke. That bein' so, the Kid may be real anxious to show us the way in."

"Hunh," Bitter Root grunted eloquently, "so that's why you bin puttin' up with him, eh? I knew there was sunthin'. . . . But can you take a chance on anythin' he says? You know we kin git over our heads in a hurry."

"I don't have to take much chance on him," Bill informed him. "I been pumpin' Cherokee right along and pickin' out of his talk the things I could believe. I've got the picture pretty well set in my mind, and I don't know that I could have got the facts any other way. What I ain't been able to learn is just where Smoke's got his lookouts posted."

"Yuh can bet your roll the Injun knows," Bitter Root remarked with positiveness. "I can't see what it'll gain him to deal from the bottom this once. It certainly won't be good for his own hide."

"That's what I'm thinkin'," Bill observed thoughtfully. "He's thick about some things, but it'll occur to him that if he ain't on the level this once that we'll git him if the other side don't. It was his idea, of course, that we wouldn't git around to this for weeks. Any plans he was makin' don't amount to nothin'. It was his brag that he wanted a showdown with Smoke. Well, I'm callin' his hand now; it's too late for him to eat his words. He'll have to play the cards he asked for."

In the deepening twilight they walked back to the fire. The men sat around, their faces tense. Cherokee had his pack of cards out and was shuffling them absent-mindedly.

"You're as glum as owls," Bill chided them. "What's eatin' yuh? No time now to let your nerves bother yuh."

It provoked an answer from only Tonto.

"I guess my nerves is all right," he grumbled. "I was just thinkin' the ten of us will hardly be settin' down to supper together tomorrow night."

"What do yuh mean!" Bill jeered. "Look at Latch and Bitter Root here! They've had the clothes shot off of 'em a dozen times and they still git around pretty chipper!"

"Did you see anythin'?" Cherokee inquired, without bothering to glance up from his cards.

"Nary a thing," Bill answered him. "I reckon Smoke is at the Meadows by now." He turned to Maverick. "Let's have that grub, Maverick. We want to be gettin' away from here in ten or fifteen minutes."

As they ate, he tried several times to break the tension that was tightening their mouths and leaving them without a word to say. He failed dismally. If he asked a question it always waited for Latch, Bitter Root or Flash to answer.

"They'll come out of it," he told himself, doubly glad, however, that he had Bitter Root and Flash with him. He glanced at the Kid and saw that he had eaten only a mouthful. "What's the matter, Cherokee, ain't yuh got no appetite?"

"Naw. . . . I'm anxious to be movin'——"

"We can be stirrin' directly. I just want to say a word or two before we pull away." Bill realized that every eye was focused on him instantly. "I figger we're about four miles from the Grocery. Is that right, Kid?"

"Just about——"

Bill glanced at his watch in the firelight.

"The moon won't be up till nearly ten. That gives us about two hours. We ought to be ready to give 'em hell by then."

"You mean you ain't waitin' for daylight?" the Kid asked incredulously.

"I should say not! We don't know how long that bunch will stall around before they rush the shanty. When they find it deserted they'll smell a mouse in a hurry."

"You said it!" Latch exclaimed. "They'll ride their broncs into the dust in their hurry to git back to the Grocery!"

"Well, let's go then!" Cherokee growled. He flung himself to his feet and started for his horse.

"Just a minute, Kid!" Bill jerked out. "We can't ride in there blind. I'm dependin' on you to show us the way. We can't afford to bump into one of their lookouts and have a shot tip our play off."

"Don't put it up to me," the Kid flung back at him. "You're the boss; you lead the way. If I tried to take you in and somethin' went wrong you'd put it up to me."

"Why should anythin' go wrong?" Bill asked, his eyes drilling holes in the Kid.

"Things have a habit of doin' that, don't they?" Cherokee snarled. "It would be pretty soft to sneak in and surround the place without them knowin' what was up. You ought to know the chances are all against it bein' done."

"I hope to tell yuh I know it! And I'll tell yuh somethin' else, Kid: we ain't goin' to surround the Grocery. We're goin' in together—in a bunch—and open up the second we're close enough to throw lead. I'll be responsible for what happens, but I don't want to step on a hornets' nest if I can help it—not that I'm thinkin' so much about my own skin."

His words worked a change in the Kid.

"Don't try to get through that ridge," he muttered, his eyes beady.

"I don't intend to try it," Bill snapped. "We'll ride due west from here. When we're beyond the Grocery we'll take to the badlands and work back. Is there anythin' wrong with that?"

Cherokee shook his head pityingly at him.

"That'll be swell, if yuh don't mind gettin' cut to pieces," he burst out. "When you git in those arroyos a ways you'll find 'em snarled with barbed wire, and the banks so steep a horse can't crawl out. If we're caught there, not a man of us will git out alive. Yuh can do as yuh please, but if it was me, I'd take the old La Junta trail."

"For what reason?" the red-haired one queried, his tone purposely contemptuous.

"Because it's out in the open! We won't have a bit of cover, but if the other fellow sees us we at least can see him!"

Little Bill hesitated for only a moment over his decision. He could not hope to get more out of Cherokee.

"All right, we'll take the trail!" he jerked out. "Keep your eyes peeled and your head workin', and don't bang away at the first thing that moves!"

Chapter XXI

THEY reached the old La Junta cut-off without incident worth mentioning. Danger to themselves began now as they headed north.

"We'll walk our ponies," Bill advised. "Don't want any drummin' of hoofs to give us away."

Off to their right half a mile, the ridge began to rise. The trail paralleled it almost to the Kansas line. Cherokee flicked anxious glances at it. He was riding between Bill and old Bitter Root. They sensed his agitation.

"I wouldn't begin worryin' yet about anybody jumpin' us from that direction," the former remarked. "The night's still black; if there's anybody up there they can't have seen us."

"I reckon you're right," the Kid drawled. "If Smoke's got us spotted he'll let us git pretty well into the Grocery before he shows his hand." He rolled a cigarette and stuck it between his lips. "We'll be in a bad way if that happens; we'll have hell front and rear—" He raised his hand to snap a match against his thumb nail.

"Don't light that match!" Bill rasped. "That goes for the bunch of yuh!"

"Why, we're still two miles from the Grocery," Cherokee growled.

"That may be so," Bill retorted, "but we ain't strikin' a light! It might be just as well to end the talkin' too."

They went on warily. Twenty minutes later they topped a low rise. Half a mile away yellow daubs of light outlined the windows of Black Grocery. To the east, beyond the ridge, the moon was giving evidence of its coming.

Little Bill got their attention with a whispered word.

"We'll just go on easy as we have been," he said. "It'll be light enough to see a ways in a few minutes. We can size things up then."

They had not proceeded a hundred yards when Cherokee flung his rifle to his shoulder and fired instantly at something off in the darkness just ahead.

"Damn your hide!" Bill cursed him. "Didn't I tell yuh not to bang away like that?"

The Kid fired a second time. Below them they heard a man groan as he fell heavily. A horse dashed away.

"I dropped him," the Kid muttered. "I knew what I was shootin' at that time. I wasn't any too quick."

It put quite a different face on things. Bill forgot his anger.

"I reckon yuh couldn't do nothin' else," he exclaimed. "No use tryin' to creep up now. There go the lights! They know what it means!"

They saw that he spoke the truth. Upstairs and down every light had been extinguished. The Grocery and the barns across from it bulged blackly through

the darkness. Along the ridge, however, the moon was
touching the trees with silver.

"Come on!" Bill cried. "We'll swing off to the left
and come up behind the barns!"

The words were hardly uttered when a rifle spurted
flame from a darkened window. As though answering
a signal, a gun crashed, high on the ridge. In a second
or two there was a savage burst of gunfire from the
roof of the Grocery. They were shooting blindly, but
they waited only for the moon to bathe the valley in its
soft, silvery glow to give them a target.

"Don't no one pull a trigger!" Bill shouted to his
men. "They don't know where we are and we don't
want 'em to!"

It was growing lighter every second. Even at a driving gallop it seemed to take them forever to get the
barns between themselves and the store.

They made it, however. Bill glanced at them. They
were all there.

"Scotty, you and Maverick hold these horses!" he
barked. "The rest of yuh rip a board off this barn! We
got to git through here!"

Prying the boards off with their rifle barrels, they
made short work of getting inside the barn. They
brought their horses in with them and stabled them
alongside the Sontag string.

Across the away, a man bounced out of the door and
started for the barns. Latch dropped him in his tracks.
It brought a crashing fusillade from a dozen guns.
Slugs screamed all about them, splintering the stable
partitions and thudding dully into the timbers of the

barn. Bitter Root cursed as one slapped the dust out of his vest.

"Push somethin' up there and barricade that door!" Bill commanded hoarsely. "They'll rush us any moment now!"

Bags of oats were stacked high in a corner. They toppled the pile over so it fell across the doorway. Link and Maverick grabbed one end of an old wagon box; Scotty and Tonto caught up the other end. Together they tossed it on top of the bags of oats. It made an excellent barricade.

Sprawled out behind it they began to pour a murderous fire into the store. It went unanswered for a moment. From around a corner of the building then eight men appeared. A little, bandy-legged man, a six-gun in either hand, led them in a concerted rush at the barn.

"It's Little Arkansaw!" Bitter Root screeched. "I'll handle him!" Disdaining the protection of the barrier, he stood up and began to pump his rifle.

From the rooms above the store came a rain of gunfire. A slug hit an iron strap on the wagon box and glanced off to tear a ragged hole through Bitter Root's right shoulder. He shook himself like a terrier, and, undaunted, continued to blaze away. A blood-curdling yell burst from his lips as he saw Little Arkansaw go down and roll around in the dust.

Little Bill and the others were firing rapidly. The men who had dashed around the corner of the store held their ground doggedly for a minute or two, though it passed belief that any of them could escape being hit. Aside from Little Arkansaw, who had evidently been left in charge, they may never have figured importantly in Smoke Sontag's plans, but they could fight. One of them bent down to pick up Little Arkansaw. A bullet smacked him. A leg buckled under him. He grabbed Little Arkansaw, however, and dragged him out of the line of fire. The others retreated with him.

"We stopped that!" Bill ground out fiercely. He looked his men over. Scotty Ryan lay stretched out on the floor. Bill flung himself down beside him. "Scotty —where did they git yuh?"

There was no answer. Scotty's hair was matted with blood.

"He ain't bad hurt!" Bill exclaimed after a hasty examination of the wound. "Somebody toss a bucket of water on him!"

It had the desired effect. Latch wrapped a shirt sleeve around Ryan's head.

"See what yuh can do for Bitter Root!" Bill muttered.

"I don't need none of yore fussin'!" the old man grumbled. "I'm still goin' strong! It was a woman got me from thet corner window up there, damn her hide!"

"I noticed that," Bill ground out. "There's two or three of 'em up there. They been doin' all that shootin'. I draw the line at turnin' my guns on a woman, but——"

"But nuthin'!" Bitter Root growled. "The hissin', spittin' cats, they're wus then any man yuh ever faced! Right when the shootin' was the heaviest I saw one of 'em toss her empty rifle away and stand there and throw a water pitchur at us! Wimmen like them will cut yore heart out!"

"I'll put a stop to that," Bill promised. "It won't take me long to git 'em out of there."

"What do yuh aim to do?" Cherokee queried. The firing had ceased momentarily.

"I'm goin' to smoke 'em out," Little Bill snapped. Cupping his hands to his mouth, he shouted: "I'm givin' yuh two minutes to git your women out of there! I'm touchin' a match to the Grocery!"

"Go to hell!" a voice screamed back at him.

Bill had his watch out. His face was stony. The Kid wormed his way back to him.

"Say, you're bluffin' about this, ain't yuh?" he snarled. "The Grocery is worth money to us!"

"Our hides is worth a lot more," Bill answered him. "This thing has been a stand-off so far. The minutes are clickin' away. First thing we know we'll have Smoke's bunch tearin' into us. I said I'd give that crowd across the road two minutes—and I meant it!"

"That's just two minutes too long!" Cherokee cried. "There's a cellar under the rear of the store. Like as not they've got horses there. They can go out that way and give us the slip while we stand here gabbin'——"

"The Kid's right!" Luther exclaimed. "They've pulled out and set the place afire themselves!"

"They have for a fact!" Latch cried. "That's flames lickin' along the roof!"

Bill put his watch away. The two minutes were up.

"Come on!" he ordered. "We'll find out whether

they've pulled away or not! Bitter Root, you stay here with Cherokee and Scotty. Luther and Maverick will go round one side of the store with Latch. The rest of yuh come with me."

They darted across the road without a shot being fired at them. A few seconds later they met in the rear of the store. Two horses were tethered in the open cellar. Fresh droppings told them that six or seven horses had been quartered there a few minutes ago.

"They're gone, all right!" Luther got out breathlessly. He started into the cellar only to have Bill stop him.

"There's one of 'em that didn't git away," the red-haired one muttered.

"Yeh, he'll never be no deader," Latch declared, turning the body over with his boot. "By the looks of things some of the rest must be pritty well shot up."

"Well, watch yourselves!" Bill exclaimed. "We're goin' in. If we can beat that fire out we'll do it."

"Why bother?" Luther demanded. "We ain't no better off here than we are across the road as long as that barn stands there!"

"There's nothin' to stop us from burnin' the barn down," Bill told him. "She'll go in a hurry. We can hold off fifty men then."

Bill led the way up to the first floor of the store. The moonlight pouring in through the shattered windows enabled them to see well enough.

"What's that?" Link gasped, freezing in his tracks. From above came a thudding, scraping sound. It stopped for a moment and then began to move down the stairs.

"Stand back!" Bill warned tensely as he stuck out a foot and pushed the door open. A low gasp of astonishment broke from his lips as a woman backed down out of the smoke-filled stairway. She was dragging Little Arkansaw's dead body.

She straightened up with a scream of hatred as she caught sight of them.

"You wolves," she cried viciously, "you killed my man! I hope you rot in hell for it!"

Without warning she sprang at Luther and tried to wrest his rifle out of his hands. Latch pulled her away.

"Give her a hand with that thing, Maverick, and git her away from here!" Bill ordered. "Look out she don't pull a knife on yuh!"

He ran up the stairs to the second floor. The others followed. One corner of the roof was ablaze, the flames eating down through the ceiling and one of the side walls.

"We can put that fire out on the roof!" Bill told them. "Soak some blankets and crawl up this ladder with me; Luther, you git an axe or two and knock down that side wall! You'll have to move fast!"

In a few minutes they had the blaze on the roof under control. As they worked, the firelight made them easy targets. Not a shot was fired, however, those of Smoke's men who had not been wounded having evidently ridden off to meet him.

"How yuh makin' it down there?" Bill called to Luther.

"We got the fire blocked off!" Luther answered. "If yuh can spare a man or two we'll beat it out!"

"I'll git the boys from the barn!" Bill ran to the front of the building and got Cherokee's attention. "Git the horses out of there and set that barn afire!" he shouted. "Yuh can put our string in back of the store! Git up here then! We need yuh!"

He stood there a moment, wondering whether Scotty and Bitter Root were in any shape to give the Kid a hand. He had almost instant proof of it as the three men hustled the horses out of the barn. Bitter Root and Scotty rode out then, leading Six-gun and the rest of their own ponies. The Kid was evidently busy firing the barn.

The two men did not wait for him. As they disappeared around the side of the store it was still for a moment. With a start, Bill realized that here was a chance for Cherokee to pull out. His jaws clicked together grimly as the thought burned into his brain. Rifle trained on the barn door, he waited.

The Kid seemed to be a long time about it if he were only firing the hay.

"He could slip out the back way," Bill muttered.

He listened intently. A sound reached his ears. At first he thought it came from directly to the rear of the barn. He caught it again, however, and realized that it was the distant drumming of driving hoofs. He narrowed his eyes in a piercing squint but could see nothing. It was not necessary to have the proof of his eyes to know what it meant.

"It's Smoke!" he droned.

Suddenly below him the barn burst into flame from one end to the other. Cherokee ran out into the road. The roaring flames crowded out all other sounds.

"Come on, git up here, Kid!" Little Bill yelped at him. "I'm waitin' for yuh!"

Chapter XXII

BILL ran back to the others with his news. Working feverishly, they extinguished the fire in the wall.

"Four men up here is enough!" he exclaimed. "Luther, you and Link and Flash stay with me! The rest of yuh git downstairs! Do as Latch tells yuh! They won't come at yuh from the front until the fire burns down! Just watch the rear and the cellar! We'll be all right if the barn don't set this place to burnin' again."

The blazing barn was lighting up the plain half the way to the ridge.

"Be ready for 'em when they first show up," Bill advised the three men who remained with him. "They'll come too far, not realizin' we can see 'em. We'll take advantage of that mistake."

With the constant fear that flying sparks from the barn would ignite the store to disconcert them, they waited with nerves taut.

"There they are!" Flash announced. "The whole bunch of 'em!"

"Let 'em come on!" Bill cautioned. "That's Smoke ahead there. Grat's just in back of him. I don't see nothin' of Beaudry."

"I do. . . . He's over there nearest the ridge," Luther muttered. "He's pullin' up, too! Knows they're seen, I reckon!"

Bill had a brief glimpse of the man Luther indicated.

"It's him, sure enough!" he acknowledged, his mouth hard. "He's droppin' back so far I'm losin' sight of him——"

"They'll all be droppin' back directly," Flash declared. "We better take a crack at 'em before it's too late."

"Wait," Bill insisted. "They won't turn around until they've thrown a little lead at us. We'll let 'em have it when we see 'em raise their rifles."

He could count only thirteen men, including Beaudry, who had disappeared in the direction of the ridge.

"That's what I make it," Link agreed. "Unless Beaudry's got some reinforcements back there we ain't outnumbered much."

The roof of the barn fell in, sending up a shower of sparks that fell all about them. One, as large as a man's hand, ignited the tar paper roof. Link scrambled to his feet to put out the flame. Bill yanked him down roughly.

"Don't do that!" he stormed. "Get careless like that and you'll be picked off! Crawl over there on your hands and knees, and keep your head down!"

For a few seconds after the barn roof had fallen in, the flames leaped higher than ever. The Sontags reined in their ponies sharply, obviously realizing that they stood revealed, but before they wheeled around they flung their guns to their shoulders, as Bill had foreseen, and began to pump them savagely.

Apparently taking it for granted that the enemy was posted on the roof, they spattered it with lead.

"Let her hum," Bill cried, "and make her count!"

As they pushed their rifles over the edge of the roof they discovered that the fire cast a highlight on the front sights that made it difficult to draw a fine bead on anything. They fired, however. A shot or two, and they had the range.

"I dropped one of 'em!" Flash yelled. "D'yuh see him pitch out of his saddle?"

"It looked like Shorty Pierce!" Link muttered. "I made one of 'em grab his belly! Be damn strange if we didn't muss up a couple of 'em!"

Bill and Luther were centering their fire on Smoke and Grat, but the two Sontags seemed bullet-proof. Both had slid to the ground and were firing over their saddles.

A second or two later another one of their men threw away his gun and clutched his saddle horn to steady himself. It decided the issue temporarily in Smoke's mind. With agility, remarkable in a man of his size, he flung himself into his saddle and headed for the ridge, the others pounding along behind him.

"Finally tumbled that he wa'n't gittin' anywhere, I guess," Flash chuckled. "This fight is gittin' down to where it's man for man."

"Yeh, and without any help from me!" Bill raged. "I never put a mark on either one of the Sontags, and you didn't do any better, Luther!"

"I know it," Luther grumbled. "I ain't got no excuse to offer. I sure was holdin' on 'em dead center. . . ."

But this shindy ain't over; they won't be so lucky the next time."

Ten minutes passed without the attack being renewed.

"Waitin' for the fire to burn out," Link observed.

"No, they won't wait that long," said Bill. "The fire is some advantage to 'em, and they'll use it. The thing for us to do is to git downstairs. When they come at us it will be front and rear. You see if they don't."

"I hope they try it," Link rasped. "There's light enough out in front for us to see 'em for three hundred yards."

"That's what they'll figger on," Bill argued. "They'll hope to make us think that's the direction the fight is comin' from. It'll be just a bluff to draw us away from the rear. That's where your real fight will be!"

Downstairs he found only Bitter Root and Tonto in the store proper; Latch and the others were in the back. They had broken out the windows and piled sacks of flour shoulder high in front of them.

"How does it go?" Cherokee asked.

They hung on Bill's words as he gave them a brief account.

"Then they can't have over nine or ten men left," Latch declared.

"Not unless Beaudry shows up with a bunch," Luther volunteered.

"I hope he does!" Bill ground out. "I'm just afraid he's pulled out of this fight. If yuh don't see him when they come at us this time yuh can take it for granted that he's gone."

"He may be smart at that," the Kid drawled. "The way things are goin' there won't be much left of the Sontag gang by daylight."

The prospect seemed altogether to his liking.

"There'll be plenty of it left as long as Beaudry's alive!" Bill muttered tonelessly.

A warning cry from Bitter Root stopped him from saying more.

"They're comin' this way!" the old man yelled. "We see one or two of 'em!"

"I'll be back directly!" Bill exclaimed as he started for the front. "You watch things here and be sure yuh got that cellar door blocked!"

He found Bitter Root and Tonto stretched out behind some boxes of goods. Bitter Root's right arm hung limply. He had his rifle propped up, however, and was ready for action.

"Where did yuh see 'em?" Bill asked.

"Off there to the south," Bitter Root told him. "They swung around now so that the side of the buildin' shuts 'em off."

"Bill, they can't mean to come at us this-a-way, can they?" Tonto asked tensely.

"No, just a feint, I figger." He stretched out beside Bitter Root. "We'll be ready, no matter what happens."

Three or four minutes dragged by. Across the way the fire was slowly dying down. An acute sense of misgiving began to clutch Little Bill as the silence continued. He could not help asking himself if he had missed a trick. Suddenly, then, a rifle barked, off to the rear of the Grocery. A second gun roared. Every few seconds then a shot rang out. Bill began to smile to himself.

"They'd have us believe there was only two men out there," he said. "There'll be a little action out here now just to drive the idea home."

True to his prediction it was only a moment before they heard a tattoo of flying hoofs coming their way.

"Not more'n two or three," he thought.

It was a shrewd guess, for seconds later, two horsemen flashed into view. They were flattened out on the far side of their ponies, one foot in the stirrup and a hand on the saddle horn.

At the first burst of gunfire from the store, one rider swerved to the left and swung in alongside the building. The other came on, riding like a madman. Directly in front of the store he did a somersault into the dust and came up with a six-gun in either hand. With a leap he was on the store steps.

"It's Grat Sontag!" Bill jerked out.

He fired at him instantly, and knew he hit him. But Grat reached the door and dodged inside.

"He's back of that counter!" Bill yelled.

The warning was unnecessary, for the flame spurting from Grat's guns said plainly enough where he was.

Tonto was nearest him. On hands and knees he started to crawl around some barrels that stood on the floor.

"Look out!" Bill yelled. "He's got the light in back of him; he can see yuh!"

Tonto tried to pull back, but he was too late. Grat fairly riddled him. And yet, with iron courage, life running out of him like sand from an overturned glass, Tonto pulled up his gun and emptied it almost in Grat's face.

Bill had just reached the end of the counter at the front of the store, hoping to get Grat between Tonto and himself, as the former crumpled up like an empty sack. Beyond Grat, Tonto slumped to the floor.

"Tonto!" Bill cried, his voice hoarse with fear. "Where did he git yuh?"

There was no answer.

Leaping over Grat's body, Bill raised Tonto's head. A glance was enough.

"Lord," he groaned, "he's just shot to pieces!"

Bitter Root turned Grat over.

"Look at him!" he muttered. "Yuh'd hardly know it was Grat."

"I ain't worryin' about him," Bill exclaimed. "But this boy here got into this jam through me. He can blame me for this."

"Better put the blame where it belongs," Bitter Root advised calmly. "Smoke and Beaudry put this trouble on yuh. Yuh wa'n't askin' for it."

"That's my only excuse," Bill murmured, more to himself than to Bitter Root. "I'll git both of 'em for what they've done to me. If I don't do it tonight, I'll keep after 'em until I do, and I'll be thinkin' of this boy when I fetch 'em!"

He was pulled to his feet by a terrific crashing of

guns. On the heels of it came a furious and sustained barking of rifles that dwarfed anything that had gone before.

"They mean business this time," he told Bitter Root, a fury in his eyes. "I'm goin' back there. I'll have Maverick step in here to help yuh keep this end clear——"

"Don't bother; I can handle it alone——"

"I'll send Maverick just the same," Bill insisted, running to the door that led to the rear room.

He found Latch and Maverick firing from the center window.

"Where are they?" he asked, shouting to make himself heard.

"Workin' up to the buildin' from both sides!" Latch answered. "Plenty shadders back there! It's pritty hard to see 'em."

Bill edged up to the window beside him. He found the shadows just as black as Latch said they were. A hundred yards away, however, rifles spurted flame almost continuously.

"They seem to have found some cover!" he exclaimed. "There must be a ditch out there! Don't let 'em git in where they can mow down our horses!"

He got Maverick's attention and told him to go up to the front of the store. A question leaped into Maverick's eyes. Bill pretended not be aware of it.

"No use sayin' anythin' yet," he thought. "It might upset 'em."

For a quarter of an hour the firing continued without a lull. His eyes grew accustomed to the shadows, and he saw that Smoke and his men were afoot. It certainly meant that they were determined to bring the fight to close quarters.

"They're beginnin' to git a little desperate," he thought, grim satisfaction tightening his mouth "I reckon there's some of 'em won't ever git in here unless we carry 'em in feet first."

At the next window, Flash let out a yell.

"They git yuh?" Bill demanded.

"I been stung two or three times!" Flash answered. "I just knocked one of 'em end over end. That makes it okay with me!"

"Was it Beaudry?"

"Bill, he ain't in the fight, I tell yuh!" Luther shouted. "We ain't goin' to have the pleasure of settlin' with him tonight!"

"There'll be other nights," the red-haired one muttered to himself. As he reloaded his gun he felt something burn across his head. Its touch was so light it didn't even shake him. A second later, blood began to run down his cheek. "That was mighty near keno," he thought. A few seconds later, Latch stopped a slug.

"Just creased me," he grinned.

"Well, I'm goin' up on the roof and see if I can't break that up a little," Bill told him.

Leaving the window, he hurried to the stairs and climbed to the second floor. He had not yet reached the upper landing when a movement in the room off to his right halted him abruptly. The door was open. Silhouetted against the glow of the fire he saw the figure of a man outlined against the window for a moment.

The man's size alone identified him. It was Smoke Sontag!

A ladder placed against the window explained his presence there. Smoke beckoned to some one else coming up, and then passed through a door that led into the next room.

Bill stood there, helpless in his surprise for an instant. He galvanized into action then. Tossing his rifle on the bed, he drew his .44's and ran to the window. He found himself confronting the astonished face of a man climbing the ladder.

A quick heave sent the man toppling over backwards. Without wasting another glance at him, he turned to follow Smoke. The big fellow, familiar with every corner of the Grocery, was moving cautiously from room to room, evidently intent on making sure that the upper floor was unoccupied.

Finally, he stepped out into the hall.

"Steve—where are yuh?" he demanded in a loud whisper. He glanced at the window where the ladder had stood. His back was to Bill, but the latter saw him stiffen with sudden alarm. Smoke was only ten feet away. He could have killed him where he stood. Instead, he called a warning.

"Smoke—I got yuh!"

In that dreadful instant the big fellow must have realized that he was looking into eternity; that he was safe only so long as he kept his back turned. He had a gun in his hand, and he was fast with it. But so was Little Bill, and it was hardly in the cards that a man could whirl around in that narrow hall and shade him that precious fraction of a second that spelled the difference between life and death.

A strange mixture of courage and anger steadied him. His jaws clicking together with a wolfish snap, his cheek muscles bunching into little knots that distorted his face, he spun around.

It was the expected thing, utterly devoid of surprise. And yet, he got in the first shot. It might have served him better had he held it a tenth of a second and made it count, for he had no second shot coming to him.

Unhurried, Little Bill fired from the hip. His hand had never been steadier. He could have had a second shot, but there was no need for it. Smoke simply raised up on his toes, and brushing the wall, sank down as though he were being lowered by a rope.

Bill approached him warily. Believing him dead, but taking no chance, he kicked Smoke's gun out of reach. The big fellow's eyes rolled open. There was still a faint gleam of life in them.

"Smoke—yuh had this comin' to yuh," Bill said soberly. "Yuh only got a few seconds to go. . . . Tell me this—did Beaudry run out on yuh?"

Smoke's eyes said yes. He tried to speak, but his lips were leaden. Bill had to bend low to catch his faintly whispered, "You—fetch—the rat, Bill——"

"I will. . . . Yuh can count on that——"

No one ran up from below to investigate the shooting; proof enough that they had not heard it above the banging of their own guns.

Bill walked to the window. He saw the ladder lying on the ground. A glance along the building told him no one was there. He walked to the other side and inspected it. No one there, either.

Wearier than he suspected, he climbed to the roof. He peered about him cautiously. A little sigh of relief escaped him as he realized that he was alone.

"Smoke was the only one that got in," he thought aloud. He had not been sure until now.

Suddenly he froze to attention. It was only the crushing stillness that had startled him. He twitched his ears incredulously. They had not deceived him; the guns that had made the night hideous with their vituperation were silent at last.

It dawned on him slowly that the fight was over; that the shattered remnant of the Sontag gang had slunk away, never to have identity again under that name.

Minutes later, Luther and Link found him squatted down on the top step, his shoulders hunched as he sat in deep contemplation. They had just discovered Smoke's body.

"Bill," Luther cried, his voice pinched with anxiety, "are yuh all right?"

The red-haired one raised his head.

"Yeh, I'm okay, Luther," he murmured slowly, wiping his blood-smeared face with his sleeve. "It's all over, eh?"

"But Smoke—did you git him?" Link demanded.

"Yeh, it was me. . . . How did we come through?"

"We lost Tonto—maybe Flash won't pull through. The rest of us is banged up some, but nothin' serious."

"Flash got it pritty bad, eh?" Bill questioned.

"I don't figger he's up to sittin' a saddle," Luther answered. "If we're pullin' out———"

"We ain't pullin' away, Luther," said Bill. "The Grocery belongs to us now. We're stayin' right here."

"But what about Beaudry? Ain't we goin' after him?"

Bill hesitated for a moment. Then:

"I wouldn't know where to look for him tonight. But Cherokee will lead us to him some day. Yuh can be sure of that. . . ."

Chapter XXIII

THEY were comfortable, well fed and reasonably safe at Black Grocery. Long before their wounds had healed they could have had their pick of a dozen desperadoes, all good men and true, with a price on their heads, who came to the Grocery to swear allegiance to Little Bill and sought to enroll themselves under his banner, for news of the annihilation of the Sontags had traveled far, and they smelled rich pickings ahead for the Stillings boys.

Bill said no; he had men enough. He did not waste any words about it, for those case-hardened souls measured a man by the iron in his make-up. And yet, without seeming to curry favor, he won their good-will by staking a number of them to grub and ammunition. Others found it easy to turn a dollar by arriving at the Grocery with beef and ponies, of which they were by no chance the lawful owners.

Before Flash and Bitter Root were able to ride again, Bill led the others into Medora, Oklahoma, and robbed the bank without a hand being raised against them. For their trouble they got less than a thousand dollars however. But the ease with which they had accomplished the robbery emboldened them, and two weeks later they stopped a Santa Fé train, south of

Waukomis, only to find the express car bristling with deputy U. S. marshals.

Empty-handed, they returned to the Grocery, carrying Link and Luther so badly wounded that for ten days their lives hung in the balance.

They saw nothing of Beaudry, though he was variously reported to have been seen on the Canadian, and again that he was hiding in the Nations with the Chickasaws. Bill investigated the rumors and failed to find a trace of him, and as the weeks went by he was inclined to agree with Latch that Beaudry had quit the country for Arizona or New Mexico. It was a feeling that was prompted in no little degree by Cherokee's disarming lack of interest. The Kid had settled down to a life of ease and, apparently, was well satisfied with things as they were.

One morning they awakened to find a trace of snow on the ground. In that country, winter was no great hardship, but it would curtail their activities for weeks to come, for they could never tell when snow would fall. When it did, they would leave a trail behind them that a child could follow.

It forced a decision on Bill. He knew they must have money to carry them through the winter. There was only one way they could get it, and it must be accomplished without delay.

Accordingly, three days later, they rode into the little town of Sweetwater, just across the line in the Panhandle. It was an old story to them by now, and they walked out of the bank with over five thousand dollars. But as they mounted hurriedly and raced out of town, a money bag slipped off of Luther's saddle. The loss was not discovered until they had gone a block. It was too late to turn back then.

It was after daylight the following morning when they pulled up at Spirit Springs, due west of Leach Lytell's ranch. They were well out of Texas, but Lytell's enmity was something to consider.

"We better hide out here for the day," Bill decided. "Our ponies are weary. We'll take turns standin' guard while the rest git some sleep. As for Lytell, he wouldn't come at us alone. Before he can git a posse lined up we'll be on our way."

They counted the proceeds of the Sweetwater raid and discovered that they had exactly twelve hundred and thirty-nine dollars.

"That won't see us through the winter," Luther muttered bitterly. He cursed himself for his carelessness. The others were almost as excited as he about it.

"We'll take it and like it," said Bill. "We came out of this without a drop of blood bein' spilled, so don't curse your luck. We'll have to turn up somethin' else in a hurry."

His philosophic acceptance of the situation worked a change in them, and they began to look at it as he did. By the time they were ready to turn in they were jesting about it.

Bill volunteered to be the first to lay out on the knoll above the springs. In the two hours he was there he saw no one, nor did Link who followed him. In fact it was not until late in the afternoon that Luther, who was taking his turn as look-out, ran down the knoll and wakened them with word that someone was coming.

"Bill, there's an outfit headin' for the springs!" he cried excitedly. "Who do yuh think it is?"

"Why, I don't know," Bill answered, propping himself up on an elbow. "Who does it look like?"

Luther could not hold back his grin any longer.

"Why, it's Tas!" he exclaimed, as pleased as a boy. "I recognized the old Sawbuck wagon right off!"

The news unloosened their tongues as nothing had done in weeks. Already time was beginning to mellow memory of the days in which they had worked for Tascosa, and they recalled them now as an idyllic existence. Emotion stirred in them. . . . Happy, carefree days. How far they had come since then!

"I'm achin' to see the old buzzard," Link chuckled. "It'll be a pleasure just to hear him cuss again. D'yuh 'member the time Maverick jerked the wild cat and palmed it off on him for venison?"

Of course they remembered it.

"He'd a killed me if he'd caught me the night he found out," Maverick declared between bursts of laughter. "I don't know what the runnin' time is between the Kiowa Agency and the river, but I musta busted some sort of a record."

Luther and Scotty recalled other incidents, strangely precious now. With the past few months forgotten, they were soon chattering like magpies. It remained for Little Bill to break in on them.

"Boys, we can't let Tascosa ride into us this-a-way," he said soberly. "We don't know who he's got in his

outfit. Whoever they are we don't want to give 'em a
chance to start a story that Tas and us was holdin' sort
of a reunion here at Spirit Springs. You know as well
as I do that some folks might jump to the conclusion
that we hadn't met by chance."

"How could they say that?" Luther demanded
gruffly, disappointment furrowing his brow.

"Some would say it," Bill insisted, "and they'd hint
that there was a connection between us; maybe that
Tas was supplying certain information."

"Well, we owe him a better deal than that," Luther
monotoned. "If we're goin' to move we better be quick
about it; they ain't over half-a-mile out."

The others gave in grudgingly. Throwing their saddles on their horses, they were ready to leave. They
had tarried too long however, for old Tas had ridden
in ahead of his wagon, and as they started into the
brush, he hailed them.

"You better go on," Bill advised Luther and the
others. "I'll talk to him."

"What yuh runnin' away for?" Tas scolded. "Yuh
certainly saw us comin' in."

Bill told him why.

"Might be sunthin' in that," Tascosa admitted. "I'll
jest ride along with yuh down the arroyo for a few
yards. I got sunthin' to say to yuh, Bill."

Bill rode on until the old man called a halt. Tas
looked him over critically.

"Wal, yuh look natchurel," he grumbled. "I'm glad
to see yuh, Bill, but yuh can't expect me to approve of
what you're doin'."

The smile died out of Bill's eyes. "I don't approve of it myself," said he. "But I can't do any different now."

"I don't know about that," Tascosa objected. "Yuh ain't got no excuse, now that you've cleaned out the Sontags."

"I've got an excuse as long as Cash Beaudry walks this earth!" Bill retorted. "You heard anythin' of him?"

"Nary a word, nor neither will you. I take it he's left the country——"

"He'll come back if he has," said Bill. "No matter where he goes he'll be in trouble soon enough. He'll head back for Oklahoma then. . . . I'll be waitin' for him."

His argument did not impress the old man.

"See here, Bill," he exclaimed, "why don't you use a little sense? Yuh can't go on robbin' banks and holdin' up trains while you're waitin' for him. Why don't yuh give yerself up and square things the best yuh can? Yuh can go after Beaudry when yuh come out—providin' he's still drawin' breath."

"No, Tas, you're talkin' in circles," Bill murmured slowly. "I'm goin' to fetch Beaudry. I ain't goin' to let nothin' git in the way of it. I know I'll be cut down some day. When the time comes, I'll take it with a grin. But if I knew I was goin' to be killed next week I wouldn't give up this wild life for a two-by-four cell. I wouldn't last long in prison; I need the open prairie.... But you got somethin' else on your mind. When did yuh leave Bowie?"

"Last evenin'." Tas produced a plug of tobacco, and after measuring it with his eye, bit a considerable chunk out of it. "I put Martha on the train yestiday."

Bill pulled himself up with a start.

"Goin' away for a visit?" he suggested, pretending to find something amiss with a stirrup.

"No, she's leavin' Bowie for good, Bill. Her mother's brother has a big ranch out in Gila county, Arizony; Martha's goin' out to live with him. She asked me to say good-bye to yuh, should I run acrost yuh."

The red-haired one's eyes were suddenly a stone wall, but Tas saw a look of torture settle on his mouth.

"That's goin' to make it awful quiet for Doc, ain't it?" Bill queried, satisfied to say anything but what he was thinking. He saw Tascosa stare at him incredulously.

"D'yuh mean yuh ain't heard that Doc passed away last week?" the old man asked bluntly.

"Why, no——"

"He did," Tas sighed. "His heart finally got him." Without urging, he supplied the details. "That left Martha all alone—except for Paint," he concluded.

"What about him?" Bill jerked out with a scowl.

"Wal, he's up and around ag'in, lookin' for a job——"

"That ain't what I meant," Bill interrupted.

"I know it ain't." Tas lifted his Stetson and ran a horny hand through his flowing locks. "Wal, I don't suppose this will set so well with yuh, and yet yuh shouldn't complain at this late date, seein' yuh wouldn't have it no other way. But to put it in a few words, Bill, I have reason to believe that Paint will be marryin' Martha before long. Yuh can't throw a couple young people together for months, with her nursin' him back to health, without sunthin' of the sort comin' out of it."

Save for an involuntary twitching of the lips and a whitening of his cheeks under the tan, Bill met it stoically. He told himself it was no more than he had been expecting for weeks; that it couldn't have ended any other way. And yet, it dried his throat. Not the surprise of it, but its finality; the flickering out of an unsuspected spark of hope that had persisted in the face of his often repeated admission to himself that Martha Southard was lost to him forever.

"That's as it should be," he found courage to say. "They'll be happy together. Paint will make Martha a good husband. . . . I hope they don't wait too long."

"I don't know," Tas murmured thoughtfully. "I talked to Paint. He said he didn't want to rush her into anythin'. I reckon he had you in mind when he spoke. He wants to git hisself a good job too. I could use him, but he said he wanted sunthin' that would give him a chance to start a little string of his own on the side."

"He's right," Bill agreed, though it gave him another stab to find Paint Johnson so ambitious and farsighted as compared to himself.

He took his leave of Tas a few minutes later, the creaking of the wagon warning him that it was lurching down hill to the springs. A mile away, Luther and the others were watching for him. He dreaded the questions that awaited him. And yet, when he had related his conversation with Tascosa, they forbore mentioning Martha or Paint.

Chapter XXIV

BITTER ROOT and Cherokee had been left at the Grocery. Bill took the former aside soon after he and the others rode in.

"Bill, he ain't made a false move," Bitter Root said without waiting for a question to be asked. "I tell yuh, he's deep. Bein' here alone with him I tried to draw him out, but I didn't git nowhere. Yuh'd think he'd given up any idear of ever seein' Beaudry ag'in. Now, I know that don't make sense. But here he sits all the time yuh bin gone, playin' cards by hisself er readin' them mail order catylogs by the hour."

"He's waitin' us out," Bill said after a moment. "We been watchin' him too close. I'm goin' to give him a little more rope."

Following Smoke Sontag's custom, he began to post lookouts on the ridge, sending one man a little north of the Grocery and another an equal distance to the south. Every twenty-four hours they were relieved. When it came Cherokee's turn to go out, Bill spied on him from a distance. Nothing developed then, nor the second or third time.

"He's figgerin' he's watched," the red-haired one decided. "I'll give him a free hand from now on. If he starts anythin' I'll try to stop it before it gits too far."

Another week passed, and he had to admit that his strategy had failed. His patience was long, however, and he hung on.

One morning, several days later, Latch called him to a window. Coming up the old cut-off was a small band of sheep and a solitary herder. Sheep were still something of a novelty in that country. Luther and five or six others had to have a look at them. Bill put a glass on the herder.

"A greaser," he announced. "He's an old man. Walks as though he'd come a long way."

"Wal, smells like mutton for supper," Bitter Root laughed.

"No, let him go," Bill said. "He'll stop for water. If he needs a little grub, give it to him and git rid of him. You savvy Mexican, don't yuh, Kid?" Cherokee said that he did. "Well, you git out on the steps and do the talkin' to him. Find out where he's goin'."

When strangers arrived at or passed the Grocery, Bill saw to it that never more than one or two of his men were in evidence. He made them hide out this morning, taking up a position in the store himself where he could overhear what passed between Cherokee and the herder, for he had a working knowledge of border Spanish that he believed was the equal of the Kid's.

The old Mexican drew up at the store steps ten minutes later and asked for permission to water his sheep at the trough. The Kid told him to go ahead.

The old man sat down beside him, and although the

day was not warm, fanned himself with his tattered hat. He said he was all the way from New Mexico, on his way to Laguna, Kansas, where his son had a small ranch. He rolled his eyes in a hungry glance at the interior of the store, and then from an old purse shook out a few silver coins.

"Do you want to buy something?" the Kid asked him in Spanish.

The old man said he wanted some coffee. Cherokee told him to wait there, that he would get it for him, and getting to his feet, walked into the store.

"He wants some coffee," the Kid explained.

"Well, give him some," said Bill. "There's plenty in the bin."

"What'll I charge him?"

The red-haired one wrinkled his brow.

"Now yuh got me," he muttered. "How would I know what to charge for anythin'? Ask him two bits; it ought to be worth that." He glanced at the Mexican. The old man was idly drawing patterns in the dust with the long staff he carried. "Does he seem to be all right?"

"Yeh, he's shufflin' along to Laguna, Kansas," the Kid explained. He repeated his conversation with the herder. It was all as Bill had originally heard it. He watched Cherokee step out and hand the man the package of coffee, but from where he stood behind the counter he could not see that the Mexican had smoothed the dust at his feet. Nor did he catch the cryptic figures that the stick traced in the dust.

"2 — O," they read. It was not a problem in arithmetic. It was a cattle brand . . . Leach Lytell's Two Bar O brand.

Cherokee saw it and exchanged a glance of understanding with the Mexican. A slight movement of the foot and the message was erased.

Two days later the Kid went to the ridge. An hour after he reached his post he headed south for Lytell's ranch.

He was back sixteen hours later. His horse could barely stand. He wiped the foam from it and walked the pony round and round, to cool it off. With dry grass he rubbed it down.

Just before dawn he started for the Grocery, leading the animal most of the way that it might freshen up enough so as not to arouse suspicion. Luck was with him, and he put the horse in the corral without a question being asked, and then entered the store to find all of them gathered around Little Bill.

"We can't expect the weather to hold fine like this any longer," the red-haired one was saying. "If we're goin' to turn a trick we've got to git at it in a day or two."

"We sure have," Cherokee chimed in. "We're due for bad weather when the moon changes."

"Now I've been rollin' somethin' over in my mind for a week," Bill continued. "It may take your breath away when you first hear it, but I know the job can be done. The money is there; we know the town backwards; it's a short ride and plenty of cover——"

"Bill, are you speakin' of Bowie?" Luther demanded incredulously.

"You guessed it, Luther. It's Bowie I mean."

If it fell short of taking their breath away it did not miss it by much.

"Bowie ain't no different than any other place, even though we used to call it our home town," Bill went on. "If we got to hoist a bank it shouldn't make no difference to us where it's located. What we want to do is to figger out what the odds are against us."

"Bill, you're a fool for even suggestin' it!" Luther burst out angrily. "Others have tried it in the past! What did it git 'em?"

"They bungled it, Luther," Bill said calmly. "It ain't been tried in three years now. With a wide-awake sheriff on the job it ain't likely the bank's got any idea somethin' may go wrong without warnin'. They may even feel as you do that we'll keep out of Bowie 'cause we're known there."

"That ought to be reason enough, but it ain't, I see!" Luther retorted.

"Sayin' we got away with it," Link put in, "how long do yuh think it would be before we got cut down here? Why, the whole town would march out here to git our scalps!"

"I doubt it," said Bill. "No one loves a banker, Link. There ain't many people in Bowie would git excited enough to take a chance on their own hides in order to help Jim Cronin or John Slayton git their money back. But you all think it over today. If yuh come around so you see it my way we can move in a hurry. It won't be necessary to size up the town or get a line on the bank itself. We know all that right now."

"I know yuh can make it sound easy," Luther grumbled. "As a matter of fact we can git by with the money we got."

"I ain't sayin' we can't," Bill admitted readily. "I'm lookin' ahead a little. Maybe it's only a hunch, but I got the feelin' that Beaudry will turn up before spring. When I've settled with him, I'm pullin' out for old Mexico. If I haven't mentioned this before it's only because I've only settled on it since we ran into Tascosa. I figger I can start a clean slate down there. . . . I'm hopin' some of you will string along with me. I don't have to tell you it'll take money to git us there."

He had no more to say. He had never tried to win them over to his way of thinking against their wills, and he did not propose to do it now. Before the day was gone, however, they made their decision, and it was yes.

That evening as Bill and Link sat on the store steps Cherokee wandered down Black Grocery Creek. He did not go over several hundred yards. His walk seemed to be without purpose. In his hand he carried a branch he had broken off a dead willow.

He surmised that Link was watching him. But that did not worry him. It was not a difficult matter to pretend to peer into a trout hole while he printed a word in the wet sand with the willow limb. It was only a five-letter word, and it spelled

B O W I E

The Kid could not forego a grin as he started to retrace his steps. He knew for a certainty that the eyes for whom the message had been left would see it at daylight and erase it as quickly as the old Mexican had blotted out the message he had drawn in the dust.

Chapter XXV

JUST beyond the cemetery, less than a mile from town, stood Otto Hahn's tumble-down slaughter house—the same Otto Hahn of the Purity Market, whose billheads had figured so tragically in old Waco's death. There, this morning, Little Bill and the others waited. Only Maverick had been left behind to guard the Grocery.

"It's only five minutes to nine," Bill murmured, flashing a glance at his watch. "We can't be movin' yet."

A tremendous preoccupation rested heavily on them. The day had broken sharp and clear, with a pleasant tang in the air, but without exception their faces were as cold and brooding as the skies were bright and sunny.

They had a light wagon with them, hitched to a team of mules, the box filled with hay; about the quantity a rancher would take into town to feed his team. Cherokee sat on the seat, idly swinging his feet. His lips had twisted into a sneer that they might see his unconcern. Deep in his eyes, however, was unmistakable anxiety.

The details of what lay before them had been talked over at length. Each knew what was expected of him.

Bill's plans were ingenious enough to promise success. Latch, Bitter Root, Scotty and Moffet, who were not so well-known in Bowie, were to swing around town and come in from the north. The others would cross the Rock Island tracks and come in from the south. They were to meet in front of the bank. There they would find Cherokee's wagon drawn up to the curb. Their rifles would be in the wagon, under the hay. The Kid himself would be perched on a stool at the counter of the little restaurant next door to the bank, ready to go into action at the first sign of trouble.

Bill had assigned each to a position best calculated to cover the actual hold-up. He, Latch and Bitter Root were to go into the bank.

He ran over it again as they waited, although there was no need of it.

"Yuh want to watch the upper windows in the hotel," he warned. "If they open up on us from there yuh got to stop 'em."

"We will," the Kid assured him. "We don't want nothin' to go wrong on what may be our last job—" His voice had a hoarse croak.

"Why damn yore red hide anyway!" Bitter Root screeched at him. "What do yuh mean crossin' our luck by sayin' anythin' like that?"

"Aw don't set yourself afire," the Kid muttered. "You're takin' me the wrong way. I was thinkin' of what Bill told us about pullin' out for old Mexico." To himself he added: "He's goin' a lot farther than Mexico this trip."

At five minutes past nine Bill told Latch he could be moving.

"Just take it easy," he said. "You'll see us crossin' the tracks. Time yourselves then so we land in front of the bank together. We'll leave here in ten minutes."

The four men rode away, holding their ponies to a jog. Bill held his watch in his hand. Latch, Flash, Scotty and Bitter Root could be seen until they swung around some Mexican shacks at the edge of town.

Bill put away his watch and spoke to Cherokee.

"You can git your team started, Kid. And don't look back for us. We'll be right behind yuh. Just keep the mules down to a walk."

They gave Cherokee a start of several hundred yards.

On coming out of the cemetery they caught sight of him again, moving along the road that ran from Bowie to Kingfisher. It was deserted, which was unusual at that time of the morning.

"Gittin' a break," Link grunted with satisfaction.

"It looks that-a-way," Bill admitted. There was a reservation in his tone. From the direction of the depot came the long-drawn wail of a locomotive whistle. For some reason it sent a shiver down his spine. "The Guthrie train is just gittin' in," he observed.

Presently they saw the hotel bus turn into the road from the depot and head for town.

"Old Wash seems to be in a hurry this mornin'," Bill remarked thoughtfully. "He's whippin' up his team."

"That gits them out of the way for us," said Luther. He sighed heavily. "Everythin' is just as it used to be. . . . It sure looks good."

"Don't git switched off into anythin' like that," Bill said sharply. "Keep your mind on what's ahead of us. I can see Latch and them movin' our way now. This is workin' out just as I figgered."

They knew they could not go far beyond the tracks without being recognized. A lot could happen in those three blocks between the crossing and the bank.

"We better close up a little on the Kid," Bill advised as soon as they had put the railroad behind them. Glancing ahead he saw two men stare at them from in front of a barbershop, and then hurry inside.

"They got us that time," Link rasped. "One of 'em was Joe Curtain. He'd know us in hell."

Bill did not answer. A block-and-a-half down the street a man had rushed out of the bank and leaped to his saddle. He was riding toward them now at a driving gallop.

Even at first glance there was something familiar about the rider. A few seconds later Bill recognized him.

"Good Lord," he groaned, "it's Paint Johnson! . . . What's he buttin' into this for?"

Before anyone could answer him, Paint yanked his horse to its heels in a slithering stop that forced the Kid to pull his team to the side of the road.

"Bill, turn around!" he yelled, his face bloodless in his excitement. "Get out of here as fast as you can!"

"You keep out of this!" Bill barked at him. "You don't belong in this play! I got no time to talk to yuh now!"

"You got to listen to me!" Paint insisted. "You've been framed!"

"What?" Without another word Bill slid to the ground and reached for his rifle under the hay. He couldn't find it. Not a gun was there. As he stood there helpless with consternation for a moment Cherokee lashed his mules into a run. "Paint—who did it?" the red-haired one finally was able to ask.

"That rat there for one!" Paint cried, jerking his head in the direction of the fleeing Cherokee.

"So he *meant* this was our last job; Bitter Root didn't misunderstand him a bit!" The thought seared its way through Bill's brain. That Cherokee must have dumped the rifles as he drove through the cemetery was not important now. To stop him—to end his crookedness forever—that was what remained to be done.

Cherokee had thrown himself flat on the seat, knowing his life hung by a thread. Bill's first shot straightened him up. In a desperate effort to save himself, the Kid leaped down, hoping to dart in between the buildings. He was too late. He was dead when his feet hit the ground.

Paint did not have to tell them that Heck Short and five deputy marshals were in the bank; that across the way Kin Lamb had a man posted at every window, for as Cherokee went down a withering blast of gunfire swept the street. Latch, Flash, Scotty and Bitter Root were still a few yards from the bank. They saw Flash pitch out of his saddle as the first shots rang out.

Hard on the heels of them, Heck and his Guthrie men swarmed out of the bank, their guns smoking. Latch, Scotty and Bitter Root, caught without rifles, could only whirl their horses and ride for their lives. Whether they made it or not, Bill and the others could not tell.

"We got to be goin' ourselves!" Paint was urging. His plea finally registered on Little Bill's mind.

"Yeh, we got to be goin'." The voice was hardly recognizable as his own. He glared fiercely at Paint. "You git off the street before yuh git mowed down! Yuh ain't goin' with us!"

"Yes, I am! They saw me stop you! They know I tipped you off!"

It was true. And the pity of it! Thought of Martha flashed in Bill's mind. How easy it was for the law to get a grudge against a man!

"All right, fan your broncs!" he cried.

"We ain't got a chance!" Luther groaned. "They can mow us down without ever gittin' in range of our six-guns!"

They were riding furiously. Behind them, bullets began to kick up familiar puffs of dust. Ahead of them, they saw Fate turn another card against them, as a slow-moving freight rolled out of the Bowie yards and straddled the road.

"That's our finish!" Link raged.

"Not yet!" Bill shouted back. "That train will save our lives if we can ride around it! Follow me!"

Dangerous though the going was for their horses, they raced alongside the moving freight with speed unabated. A veritable hail of slugs was whining about their ears and slapping into the sides of the cars.

In some way they survived it until they were halfway down the length of the train. Luther was the first to be hit. He weathered it and rode on. A few seconds later Link got it.

Out of the corner of his eye Bill saw him grab his saddle horn.

"Did they git yuh bad, Link?"

Link did not answer. His hands had dropped and he was slumping forward. Bill caught him or he would have fallen.

"You can't do nothin' for him!" Luther cried. "He's gone!"

Still Bill hung back, vainly holding on to Link.

"Bill, you're throwing your life away!" Paint pleaded. "I tell you he's gone!"

Reluctantly Bill let go. Without looking back, he rode on. This might be the end for Luther and Paint. He told himself it must not be the end for him. He still had his score to settle with Beaudry.

It had taken them only a matter of several minutes to circle around the train. It had seemed a lifetime. Now that they had the freight between themselves and Short's posse they were safe temporarily. The train began to gather speed, but it carried them well out of Bowie before they turned off to the west.

The Strip lay ahead of them, but they knew better than to believe they would be safe, once they reached it. Heck had them on the run now, and he would hang on until he climbed the very steps of Black Grocery.

"That'll be the first place he heads for," Bill brooded. A curtain of fire seemed to burn in his brain. Every few seconds he glanced at his brother. Luther caught him at it and read his thought.

"No gittin' over this, Bill," he said. "They got me through the lungs. I can make it as far as the Grocery though and give Maverick a chance to pull out. You and Paint better start headin' for the Canadian."

"We'll pull up when we git to the Meadows," Bill answered stonily. "I want to talk to Paint."

Chapter XXVI

"It ain't any mystery about how I tumbled to this business," Paint volunteered. "Lytell owed me some money. I needed it, so I went down to get it. Knowin' Lytell, I figured I might have some trouble collectin'. For that reason I thought it might be wise to look things over before I rode up to the house. That's exactly what I was doin' when I saw Cherokee step out of the kitchen with Lytell. The Kid got away in a hurry, and I could tell easy enough that he was mighty anxious not to be seen."

"When was this?" Bill demanded, his eyes blazing.

"It was two days ago. Naturally I asked myself what the Kid was doin' there—knowin' he was ridin' with your bunch. My first hunch was to get in touch with you——"

"If you only had, Paint!" the red-haired muttered bitterly.

"If I didn't it was because I settled down to watch the 2-Bar-O house. I couldn't believe Cherokee had come there just to see Lytell, and early the next mornin' I proved it, for after the men rode off for the day's work, there was Cash Beaudry, sunnin' himself on the back steps!"

Bill's mouth fell open in astonishment and he could only stare speechlessly at Paint for a moment.

Luther lifted a whitening face.

"That makes it easier for me, Bill," he murmured. "Yuh know where he is now. I'll go on to the Grocery, as I said. I couldn't be any help to yuh. I know yuh can handle him alone."

"Wait . . . there's more to this, Luther. Let Paint finish."

"I didn't know just what to do then," Paint confessed. "I thought Beaudry might pull away as Cherokee had done. I made up my mind I'd follow him if he did. But he stayed there until late afternoon. A man rode in then. He was a stranger to me. It wasn't but a few minutes before Lytell and Beaudry saddled their horses."

"Which way did they go?"

"They headed north, Bill. I followed 'em for hours. When they crossed the Cimarron I took it for granted that they were makin' for Bowie . . . I was both right and wrong about that."

"What do you mean?" Bill whipped out. "Did yuh lose sight of 'em?"

Paint shook his head.

"Here's what happened: Lytell and Beaudry got their heads together for a minute or two. Lytell went on then; Beaudry pulled up in the brakes. It was plain enough to me that he was to wait there for Lytell."

"Yuh think he's there now?" Little Bill's voice was harsh with eagerness.

"I've no reason to think he ain't," Paint answered.

"I can understand the whole deal. Lytell was in Bowie last night. It was him that tipped off the sheriff."

"No doubt of it," Bill sighed heavily. "I always figgered that Cherokee would lead me to Beaudry, but I never expected it to be this-a-way. . . . If I'd only known!"

"I tried to reach you, Bill," Paint declared, a queer little break in his voice. "I started for Black Grocery last night. I had trouble findin' my way, but I got there a little after dawn. I had a time gettin' anythin' out of Maverick until I told him what was up. Knowin' you were bein' framed—that you didn't have a chance if you went into that bank—I started back for Bowie. I didn't know where to look for you—so I went to the First National and stalled around for a minute or two. I was there when Short and his Guthrie men piled out of the bus and walked into the bank. I came out then, and there you were, ridin' up the street. . . ."

Bill nodded. He saw it all now.

"No use tryin' to thank yuh," he murmured woodenly. "You've got yourself in a jam on our account."

"I wouldn't do it any different if I had it to do over," Paint insisted. "I haven't forgot what you did for me."

"Well, that's all right in its way, but maybe it would have been better if you'd thought more of Martha and less of me before you got yourself mixed up in this. Now I need yuh; you've got to show me where that snake is hidin' out."

"I can do it," Paint promised.

"Then don't waste no time about it," Luther spoke

up. He urged his horse ahead, anxious to escape any farewell. He knew this was good-bye forever, but he was not equal to having it put into words.

It was doubly true of Little Bill. There was a stricken look in his eyes as he watched Luther move away.

"Maverick will hitch a team and git yuh to Leflett's place," he called after him. "I'll see yuh there . . ."

He knew he was lying. Maverick would never have to put Luther in a wagon and start for Jake Creek. The end was nearer than that.

Without turning, Luther raised a hand in a feeble farewell. Precious as the minutes were, Bill stood there watching him until an intervening ridge hid him from view.

"I guess we can ride," he muttered huskily. "We got quite some miles to go."

Several times they had reason to believe they were pursued. From a distance they saw groups of horsemen, proving that Heck was combing the prairie thoroughly. The forlorn hope that he might find Bitter Root and the others flickered out in Bill's mind when noontime came and they had not been seen.

"Trapped or shot down," he brooded. "The law caught up with a lot of us today."

He glanced anxiously at Paint's pony, a young bay that was beginning to falter under the driving pace Six-gun set.

"That bronc won't last much longer," he exclaimed.

"We haven't far to go," Paint answered. The tree-choked river bottom had been in sight for some minutes. "We might better drop down to the river and follow the brakes."

Half-a-mile more, and Paint identified the place where Beaudry and Lytell had crossed the river.

"All right," Bill snapped. "Now you git, Paint! Cross the river and keep on for the line!"

As Paint started to demur, a rifle cracked without warning. The bullet lifted Bill's hat from his head.

"Into the brakes!" he yelled at Paint. "He's up there on that bare knoll!"

Beaudry wasted a clip of cartridges on them without inflicting any damage.

"You think he recognized us?" Paint asked. He was as calm as Bill.

"He went after me first, didn't he? He can see in all directions from up there. He must have had us spotted for some time, figgerin' if he waited he couldn't miss at eighty yards."

"He didn't miss by much," Paint reminded him. "I don't see how you can smoke him out of there."

"I can, with just a little help from you," Bill told him. "I don't want yuh to take a hand in this fight. All I'm askin' is for yuh to swing wide around the knoll and when you git there, fire your gun every so often. It'll let him know we've split up. It'll divide his attention. That's the best chance I can hope for."

Paint tried to drive home on him the folly of facing Beaudry with only a pair of six-guns.

"Put a rifle in your hands and I'd say you might make it. I can't see it this way."

"I'll make the most of the tools I've got," the red-haired one muttered grimly.

Twenty minutes passed after they had parted before he heard Paint's gun barking. He answered the shots. As stealthily as a wildcat, he crept out of the brakes and began crawling through the brown buffalo grass that swept up to the crest of the knoll.

The light wind that blew down the river was continually fanning the tall grass. As it rose and fell in undulating waves, Bill moved through it, knowing the movement he made would be hard to distinguish from the playfulness of the wind.

Paint's gun sounded again, nearer this time. Bill cursed him for a fool.

"I told him not to take a hand in this," he groaned.

Beaudry's rifle began to speak. Paint had drawn his fire. Bill calculated the distance to the top. He still had thirty-five yards to go.

"Still too far," he decided. "I can't run at him yet. He'd drop me before I got halfway to the top."

The thirty-five yards became twenty. Bill lay there for minutes, not moving a muscle. Ahead of him the grass thinned.

"I'll lay here until Beaudry bangs away in Paint's direction again," he told himself. "I'll take it on the run then. If he drops me before I git him he'll be movin'."

A few seconds later Paint drew fire once more. His legs flying, Bill leaped for the top. Beaudry's surprise was complete, but the ill luck that had followed the red-haired one all day still pursued him, and as he leaped over the outcropping at the top he half slipped. Before he could catch himself, Beaudry's high-power sent two slugs through him that tore a great, gaping hole in his stomach.

Beaudry's rifle snicked a third time on an empty shell. He hurled the rifle from him and reached for his .45's.

A grin spread over Bill's graying face. Here was a second that was all his—a second in which to make everything right. First with one gun and then the other he wrote finis to Beaudry's plotting.

Cash moved his lips grotesquely as he sank down, but no sound came from them. His mouth had lost its sneer. The wide, staring eyes no longer held their look of cunning.

Clutching his belly, bent nearly double with agony, Bill shuffled across the knoll. Paint poked his head cautiously over the rim to find him staring down at Beaudry's lifeless body.

"You fetched him, eh?" he gasped, finding it beyond belief.

"Yeh . . ."

Paint's eyes widened with horror suddenly.

"Bill . . . Bill, he's got you too! Look at you!"

"That's all right, Paint," the other murmured slowly. "It's all right now." He raised his head and glanced about him. "Just help me sit down, will yuh. . . . Yuh can prop me up against that rock——"

Paint made him as comfortable as he could.

"You've got to let me do somethin' about this," he

said tragically. "I can bind you up so you won't bleed so much. . . ."

Bill shook his head. "No, Paint; I'll last longer if yuh don't touch me. Just pull off my boots——"

"Don't talk like that!" the other scolded. "You'll pull through this, Bill. You've got to. I don't know what you've been told, but Martha loves you. I know that's why she's makin' me wait. Think of her——"

"I *am* thinkin' of her," the red-haired one murmured softly. All the harshness was gone from his voice. "It makes this easier for me. . . . I see it was the best thing could have happened."

"Don't say that, Bill! Please——!"

"It's the truth. I knew I'd git it some day. I didn't expect it quite so soon though. No need to feel bad on my account, Paint; I ain't kickin'."

"I know you ain't. . . ." Paint turned his head away to hide his emotion. "You got every right to kick."

"No, I ain't. Outlaw is only another name for a fool!" he jerked out fiercely, his eyes burning with their old fire for a moment. "You can see what happens to 'em: Link and Luther gone; the rest of us shot up; and not a cent to show for it. Let it be a lesson to you, Paint. The law ain't got no real grudges ag'in you yet. You git yourself to a new country; stay away from the wild bunch and find yourself a good job. I want you to go straight, even though yuh got to ride through hell to do it, 'cause Martha will be waitin' for you."

Unashamed, Paint choked back a sob. On the ridge,

a mile to the east, four mounted men had appeared. He pointed them out to Bill.

"All this shootin' has been heard a long way," he got out with an effort.

Bill eyed the distant riders for a moment.

"Posse," he murmured, his face damp with perspiration. He was suffering untold agony. "Time for you to be goin', Paint."

"Bill, I ain't leavin' you. . . ."

"Yes, you are. You're goin' to let me have my way about this. I want you to take Six-gun. I said once that nobody would ever ride him but me. Well, he's yours now. Folks will tell you them claybanks are bad luck. When they do, just remember he got me here in time to fetch that snake over there." He fumbled with a belt he wore under his shirt. "You'll need some money, Paint. There's two hundred dollars here. Won't you take it?"

"I better not." Paint had difficulty getting the words out. "I don't know what lies ahead of me, Bill, but I'll feel better if I try to get there on money that hasn't got a gun behind it."

Far from taking offense, the red-haired one nodded approvingly.

"I'm glad you said that," he declared, "I know you'll make it now. But you don't have to be afraid of this money. It's wages that Tas owed me. I hope it will see yuh through."

Paint took it at his urging. But he did not offer to leave. The posse was nearer.

"Don't make me beg yuh," Bill pleaded. It was becoming more and more difficult for him to speak. "Just hand me Beaudry's rifle and some ammunition; then you slip down through the grass and git across the river."

Paint put the gun in his hands.

"So long. . . ." Bill breathed feebly. Even so it was a command. "You've only got a minute or two. I'll hold 'em back for yuh."

"So long. . . ." Paint echoed, the words choking him. In a second or two the grass hid him. Bill did not catch sight of him again.

It did not seem possible that the posse had glimpsed him either, but they were urging their horses to a gallop.

Bill fired harmlessly over their heads. He had no quarrel with these men now. It wasn't necessary to hit them to slow them up, It was just as well, for the front sight of the rifle was all fuzzy in his eyes.

Before he had emptied the clip he found his hand lacked the strength to work the bolt. Eyes dulling, he groped blindly until he found one of his .44's.

"Can't give much of an account of myself . . ." he thought.

He knew the end was near. Lapsing into unconsciousness, he continued to click the trigger long after he had emptied the gun.

Heck found him a few minutes later.

"It's Little Bill," he said. There was respect for the dead in his voice. A few feet away he saw Beaudry's body. "He kept his word, Charlie; he fetched him as he said he would."

Charlie White, the deputy, nodded.

"I see he did," said Charlie. "He's got a smile on his lips."

Heck shook his head.

"You're wrong; I can't believe there's any connection between that smile and Beaudry. This boy was right about most things, Charlie. He knew his book was being closed. I'd like to think he realized it was the kindest thing could have happened to him . . . kindest for him and for the one person in this world who meant the most to him."

THE END